PROMISED LAND, PA.

PROMISED LAND, PA.

Terror Has a New Home . . .

DAVID WARREN

Acknowledgements

Throughout the last three years, many people have helped make this project a reality. Saying that, I would like to say a quick thanks to the Lord Jesus above, through whom all things are possible. I also wanted to thank Merrit Marsango and my family for all their encouragement throughout this tedious process as well as Randy Frame for his efforts.

And for all others that have helped me along the way, my sincere thanks.

David Warren

This book is dedicated to Suzanne, my real life Sara,
as well as my children Katelyn, Matthew and Noelle. Also,
a special dedication to Charlie Garrison, for without him,
this book would not have been written.

Prologue

June 7th

The early morning sun shined brightly over the vast Pocono Mountains, its rays dancing off the tops of thousands of trees below.

Mountains of snow have long since melted, leaving behind large vernal pools, a welcome haven for frogs and salamanders. The spring peeper frogs whistle their high-pitched mating call while the spotted and Jefferson salamanders flock to sphagnum moss bogs to breed.

In early May before any trees have leaves, the serviceberry trees bloom and at this time of the year the forest floor is alive with tiger lilies, mountain laurel blooms and rhododendron.

A lone bald eagle soars the sky while squirrels quickly run up and down the American beech and red maple trees far below.

A little further up the mountain, walks a herd of whitetail deer. One fawn falls behind, searching the ground for berries. In mid search the rustling of a nearby bush startles it. Sprinting off instantly, the fawn abandons its search and rejoins the group.

All is quiet for a moment. Then, clambering out from behind the bush is the American black bear. Also known as Ursus Americanus, the large omnivore raises its long snout and sniffs the air heavily. It travels deeper into the mountain, pausing now and then to munch on some highbush blueberry trees.

The black bear continues to walk solemnly through the forest, its rounded front claws scraping the rocky, thin soil. Suddenly it comes upon a clearing in the forest. In the middle of the clearing is a large, one-story stucco building. It starts to turn around when a delightful aroma fills its nostrils.

Curious, it ambles over to the corner of the building where a rather large pile of berries sits. The bear looks down at the wonderful food and then up at the large, red letters bolted onto the structure's wall.

"That spells Intech," comes a voice from behind the bear.

Before it even has a chance to turn and run, there is a whizzing noise and a sharp pain pierces the bear's left shoulder blade. It hobbles a few feet when another object penetrates the large bear's neck. It winces in pain, stumbles, and falls. It looks up at the sky, the sun shining brightly. And then darkness.

*　　*　　*

Jim Hoffer sighed loudly. "I don't like this."

Arnold Flanks looked up from the trash can he was emptying and snorted. "You don't like what?"

"I don't like *this*," Jim replied, gesturing with his hand across the room. "Take a look around you."

Even though Arnold had seen the room dozens of times, he still took a quick glance at his surroundings.

They were in a large, windowless room with bare white walls. In the middle of the room was a large table filled with microscopes. There were also other technical objects that Arnold couldn't even begin to guess at what they were or their function. Surrounding the room on all sides were huge counters. On top of the counters were various types of cages and glass aquariums. Arnold walked over to one such aquarium and looked down. Inside were several small, white mice.

They scurried all about in their glass confinement, trampling each other in the process. To his left along the far wall were several cages full of rabbits, squirrels, and chipmunks.

"So?"

"So?" Jim said. "You don't see anything wrong with this?"

"Ain't none of my business."

"Well, I didn't sign up for this. I was hired to be a maintenance man for Intech Research and Pharmaceuticals in Allentown. Not this weird, secluded place. I mean, what in the world are they doing with all of these animals?"

"Like I said, none of my business," Arnold replied, belching loudly and scratching his large stomach. "I get paid to do a job. Whether it's fixing light fixtures here or in Allentown, I really don't care. So long as I get a paycheck."

Jim, who was tall and thin and virtually the physical opposite of Arnold, continued. "Listen, I've been doing a little bit of research on some of the stuff they've left lying around—"

"You've what?" Arnold smirked. "Who are you? Columbo?"

"I'm serious! I don't understand a lot of it but—"

"That's shocking."

"But they're doing all kinds of DNA tests with something called Thalidomide—"

"Don't care, Jimbo," Arnold said.

"And you know how we're not allowed in that big section on the opposite side of the building? Do you know why?"

"No," Arnold replied, plainly bored. "But I think you're gonna tell me."

"I overheard some of the scientists when I was cleaning up that lab spill earlier—"

"You were eavesdropping?"

"Absolutely. Anyway, they were talking about larger animals they've got locked up in here. I'm not sure, but I thought I heard them say something about a bear."

"A bear, huh?" Arnold scoffed. "Listen, Jim. If I were you I'd stop worrying about DNA tests and big animals, and I'd concentrate on my job instead. Intech is a good company with good intentions."

"The road to hell is paved with good intentions," Jim said soberly.

"They're trying to cure cancer for crying out loud! Jimbo, you need to relax. Go home and get drunk or something."

Jim smiled. "Is that an Intech cure?"

"Now I'm being serious," Arnold replied sternly. "You need to relax."

"Yeah," Jim smiled after a brief silence. "Maybe you're right."

"Of course I'm right," Arnold smirked. "Because if you don't, somebody around here might just put *you* in a cage."

Even though he knew Arnold Flanks was kidding, a cold shiver still found its way up Jim's spine.

Part One

Arrival
August 21st

Chapter One

On route PA 390, the traffic was extremely heavy. Every make and model of car and truck known to man sped along at dangerous speeds. In one particular silver Dodge Intrepid sat the Walkers.

"Sara Walker, I like the sound of that," said an attractive brunette in the passenger seat. She smiled and looked down at her brand new wedding band. "Sara Walker, Sara Walker."

Steering the car, Danny Walker grinned. "You'd better like it, you're stuck with it for the rest of your life!"

"Today is August twenty-first. Isn't it hard to believe we've been married a whole day?" Sara asked with a smile.

"Yep, seems like an eternity," Danny replied, suppressing a laugh. They came to the top of a big incline in the highway. Ahead of them in the distance, above all the traffic, were huge mountains and endless rows of trees. "Oh wow, what a view."

Sara looked over at him. "It's quite beautiful, isn't it? After all these years of coming up here, it still takes my breath away."

"You take my breath away," Danny said.

"Oh, honey," Sara beamed. "How sweet."

"Not really, it's just pillow talk," Danny laughed.

Sara elbowed him lightly in the ribs. "I think we're past pillow talk, aren't we?" Sara said, letting the sunlight reflect off her diamond engagement ring.

"Yeah," Danny replied. "How long until we reach your parents' vacation house now?"

"Not long, maybe forty-five more minutes," Sara replied.

"Forty-five more minutes!" Danny said. "I've been driving for over two hours already!"

"I know," Sara replied, as if talking to a toddler. "But the Poconos is a long way from South Jersey."

"Not far enough from Jersey," Danny joked.

Even though he made that comment, Danny really did like New Jersey. He was born and raised in southern New Jersey and had never lived anywhere else. Besides moving once when his parents got divorced, he lived in the same house his whole life, until he and Sara bought a home together last month.

"Well, after we reach our exit, we have to go past all the resorts. Then after that, we have to go through the town of Canadensis."

"The town of what?" Danny asked.

"Can-a-den-sis," Sara said, speaking very slowly.

"Canadensis," Danny said. "Got it. What's there?"

"It's mostly for tourists. There are a lot of fancy restaurants and antique shops. The only thing I like is a neat candle shop they have in the middle of town, we'll have to go sometime."

"Oh boy," Danny said with fake enthusiasm. "Anyway, what's the house like?"

"It's nothing fancy by any stretch of the imagination, but also keep in mind my grandfather built it from the ground up. It's my all time favorite place in the whole world. Wait till you see, it's really cozy."

"Sounds great to me," Danny replied. "I've been wanting to come to Promised Land ever since you first told me about it."

"I just hope the house is still okay," Sara said, her smile fading.

"Huh?"

"You know, after the tornado last month."

"That's right, I almost forgot. You said it was an F-2?" Danny asked.

"Yeah, the winds were up to 157 miles per hour. It cut a path right through Promised Land State Park and crossed Lower Lake road and

North Shore Road near Sucker Brook. My dad said he heard that over five hundred people were trapped overnight in the park."

"Wow."

"My dad said even though the tornado went practically through our yard, the only damage was that a small tree fell and hit the back of the house. But as far as I know, he cleaned it up pretty good, which is more than I can say for other parts of the mountain."

"Really? Some people got it bad, huh?"

"Yes. Only two streets over from us somebody lost their roof and half their home. Surprisingly, nobody was injured. And higher up in the mountain, that took a beating too."

"Higher up in the mountain? What's up there?" asked Danny.

"Nothing really," Sara answered. "No houses that I'm aware of. There's a lot of hiking and bicycle trails, but other than that it's mostly wildlife. I haven't seen the extent of the damage yet but my dad told me there are stacks of trees lying on their sides for miles. It really is a shame. It will be a very long time before that part of the forest will be restored. Oh, here's our exit."

As Danny took the off ramp he asked, "So how are the people up here?"

"Oh, they're great," Sara replied. "At least the people I know. Most people don't live in Promised Land year round, just during the summers."

"Really? Does the town close up in the winter?" Danny asked.

"No, nothing that drastic. I'd say maybe a quarter of the people live there all year long."

"Is there enough work in the off months for those people in Promised Land?"

"Hardly," Sara answered. "Some people might be lucky enough to find full time employment in Canadensis, but most of the residents work in Allentown, which is a little over an hour away from Promised Land."

"So how crowded is it this time of the year?"

"The last big weekend will be Labor Day, but for the most part the season is winding down and people are starting to close up their houses for the winter," Sara said. "Plus, it's in the middle of the week where as most people don't come up until the weekend. We should have plenty of privacy."

"Good," Danny said with a devious smile. "I want you all to myself."

"Wait until you see the town," Sara said. "There are so many great places to go—"

"Yeah, like the bedroom!" Danny declared.

Sara smiled, "Like the State Park."

"And then into the shower," Danny continued.

"Like the gift shops, the museum and the lake where we can rent paddle boats—"

"Skinny dipping—a great idea!"

"Not a chance, pal," Sara said. "You know how modest I am."

"Oh well, there's always the bathtub!"

Sara giggled, "I give up!"

Soon they entered the town of Canadensis. They drove on, passing little shops and restaurants. "Nice little town," Danny said. "Whoa, two dollars and fifty cents a gallon! Remind me to fill up somewhere else."

"Sorry to say, but that's the going rate up here. Not to mention that's the only gas station within miles of here," said Sara. "There's the candle shop," she said, pointing to a large, green building on the left hand side of the road.

"Oh, okay," Danny said, slightly pushing on the accelerator with a smile.

"Oh, stop it," Sara laughed.

Soon they passed out of the small town of Canadensis and onto a winding, narrow road. It swirled around sharply, each turn taking them steadily up the mountain. On one side was the mountain face and on the other—an empty void. Danny whistled, "That's a long drop."

"I know," Sara replied. "This is the most unpleasant part of the trip for me. Just take your time, honey."

"No problem, babe," Danny said. "I am in control."

He continued to drive cautiously up the mountain road. After a few minutes Danny frowned as he looked into his rearview mirror.

"What's wrong?" Sara asked, noticing his reaction.

"This clown behind me is up my butt," he muttered.

Sara turned to see an old blue sedan riding dangerously close to them. "Oh, come on," she groaned. "It's George Stine, one of the permanent locals. You know how I said most of the people up here are real nice?"

"Yeah," he said, keeping his eyes on the rearview mirror.

"Well, he's not. This makes me mad. People who live up here don't think twice about this road and how dangerous it is, it's old hat to them. They never consider people who aren't familiar with it. Geeze, what's his problem?"

"I've speeded up to thirty," Danny said. "But I'm not going any faster—not on this road."

"Don't," she said. "Forget him, he can't be in that big of a hurry. He's a grumpy old man anyway."

"He lives near your house?"

"Across town on the other side of the park," she replied.

"Well, that's good," Danny said. "At least he's not your neighbor."

"Thank God," Sara agreed, looking back over her shoulder. "He's not very—" The sound of a horn broke off her sentence. Sara watched as the blue sedan's lights began to flash, the horn continuing to sound loudly.

"What's that idiot doing?" Danny exclaimed, trying to steer properly. He could see in his rearview mirror an old face behind the other car's windshield, red and angry. "He's even shouting at me! What is he, nuts?"

As if in answer to his question, the sedan quickly cut over into the left lane. "Watch out!" Sara said, fear in her voice. "He can't see around the upcoming bend! There could be a car coming, slow down and let him pass." Danny obliged and slowly applied the brakes, and the other car raced by them. As he did so, George looked over and, giving Danny an obscene gesture, roared past them and around the curve.

"What a lunatic!" Danny cried, steadying the Intrepid. "Are you okay?"

"Yeah, I'm fine," she sighed. "That was most unpleasant."

"Yes, it was," agreed Danny.

"Well, don't let him bother you," Sara said. "The rest of the people in Promised Land are not psychos."

"That's reassuring," Danny said, looking over at his new wife and smiling.

"Trust me," Sara smiled back. "That's the most danger you'll see on your honeymoon."

Chapter Two

Allan Parker sat motionless at his desk, the small fan blowing his wavy brown hair about. He was thinking back to five years ago. Back to when he was with the NYPD. With the increase in crime, things were getting really bad on the job. The one thing that made the job bearable was the friendship that had developed between Allan and his partner of ten years, Jake Bishop. His mind halted when he remembered October twelfth. Allan and Jake had just finished their patrol. It was late, they were hungry, so they decided to go to an all night deli and get some sandwiches.

Jake had been in such an upbeat mood that night. He confessed to Allan that he was going to ask his long time girlfriend Andrea to marry him. He talked about her during the ride to the store and all the way up to the entrance. He was so busy explaining how he was going to propose that they failed to notice the man with the shotgun who was in the process of robbing the store.

The chimes on the door announced their arrival. The robber turned, saw the blue uniforms, panicked and fired. Jake was smiling, talking about Andrea one second and in the next second he was falling backward, blood splattering Allan and the glass doors behind them.

Frantically, Allan turned in shock to the man standing eight yards from him. He was an older man with short-cropped hair and a leathery face. It took Allan a second to realize the man was aiming a large shotgun at him. He tried to move, but found he couldn't. His legs felt like cement and his arms went limp. The robber half smiled, raised his weapon and fired.

Allan closed his eyes, awaiting the impact, but none came. He opened his eyes, blinked and focused on the man.

The thief wasn't smiling anymore. As a matter of fact, he looked stunned. The shotgun fell from his hands and clanged onto the tiled floor. The man took a step forward, then dropped to his knees. Allan could see blood trickling from the man's mouth. Then, the robber fell over.

Standing behind him was the clerk, an elderly Chinese man. In his hand was a smoking 9 mm. "I had to," he said in very bad English. "He . . . he was going to kill you too."

Allan couldn't speak. He turned and looked down at his fallen comrade. How was it that he was alive and Jake was not? It was an awful sight and it had all happened in less than thirty seconds.

Allan later realized that he had simply frozen. In a panic situation, he didn't respond. No, not that he didn't, it was that he *couldn't*. His whole body had shut completely down. Nothing he could have done that night would have saved Jake, but his shutdown almost killed himself as well. Allan swore to himself that he would never let that happen to him again.

Shortly after that, he decided he had had enough of the city life. He needed a change and he planned to make the most out of the second chance that God had given him. He began to think about how to make it happen.

A few weeks after the shooting at the deli, Allan had to deal with another death. His favorite uncle died after a long battle with cancer.

He remembered the times that his aunt and uncle brought him and his younger brother to their summer home in Promised Land for vacation. He remembered how much he loved it there, how peaceful it was.

After his uncle had passed away, his aunt was going to put the house up for sale, saying she had no reason to go there anymore. Allan saw the chance he had been waiting for. On an impulse, Allan resigned from his job at the police department, used his savings and bought the house in Promised Land.

As all this was happening, Bob, the park ranger for Promised Land, was on the verge of retirement and when thirty-two-year-old Allan Parker came around looking for a full time job, Bob hired him on the spot, sent him for training and sort of took him under his wing. After Allan was established as the new park ranger, Bob moved to Florida. Never having been married, Allan lives contentedly as the park ranger for Promised Land, Pennsylvania.

The slamming of a screen door interrupted Allan's thought. He looked up from his desk to find the young face of Bill Darley, his deputy ranger.

"You okay?" Bill asked.

"Yeah," Allan said. "Just daydreaming. What's up?"

"I'm getting ready to check out some of the hiking trails."

"Let me know if you find another deer," Allan said, thinking now of recent events.

"I will," Bill said and turned to leave. When he reached the door, he paused. "Hey, Allan?"

"Yes?"

"What's going on with all these dead deer lately?" he asked.

"I don't know. I'm sure it's nothing to be concerned about," Allan answered. "I'll say one thing, though. I've been the park ranger going on four years now and I've never seen so many in one month. What's the count up to? Four?"

"Five. Do you think it's a bear? They were pretty chewed up," Bill asked.

"No. Black bears don't go around attacking deer. Unless they're provoked they wouldn't harm anything."

"What if they were hungry?"

"No again. In the first place, this time of year black bears eat mainly soft mast in the form of shrub and tree-borne fruits like all the highbush blueberry trees we've got growing all over the place. And in the second place only a small portion of the bear's diet is animal matter and even then it's confined to mostly colonial insects and beetles. Although I have heard of some cases in which they've been reported to raid livestock, but that's extremely rare."

"How about a grizzly?"

"Wrong part of the country, Bill," Allan said.

"I know, but I was thinking about that zoo up by Lake Wallenpaupack. Maybe they had a grizzly on display and it escaped."

Allan smiled. "What do *you* think about that?"

"Um, extremely doubtful," Bill smiled.

"Look," Allan said, standing up. "I'm sure it's nothing, just be careful, okay? Are you taking Old Betsy?"

"Of course, she's in the truck," Bill said. That was the affectionate name Bill called his Remington 12-gauge shotgun. "She goes where I go."

Bill's father used to take him hunting all the time when he was a teenager. That's when Bill fell in love with the outdoors. Three years ago his father died in a boating accident and his mother took to the bottle to ease her grief. So Bill quit college and went to work for Allan to help pay the bills.

"Okay," Allan said. "Do that, report back to me and then call it a day."

"Really? Are you sure?"

"Yes, I'm sure," Allan smiled. "Whatever you don't get done today you can finish tomorrow."

"Okay, thanks, boss, see you in a little while," Bill said as he left the office.

Sitting back down, Allan listened to the roar of Bill's truck and sighed. For the first time in a long time he wasn't dwelling on the past. He now sat and thought about the present and one very nagging question: What is happening to my mountain?

Chapter Three

After another ten minutes the road finally leveled out. "See that place up here on the right?" Sara asked, pointing to a beige structure off to their right.

"Yeah."

"That's a really neat chocolate store I want to take you to. They make anything out of chocolate-famous people, places, and even professional wrestlers. You'd get a kick out of that."

"Okay, we'll make a point to go there sometime this week," said Danny.

"Good, I promised our families some Pocono style fudge. Oh and up here on the left is the pretzel place I've told you about," Sara said.

"Pretzel place?"

"Yeah, remember I told you that they make the pretzels right in front of you and how they have all those different kinds of popcorn?"

"Popcorn too?"

"Yes, popcorn. They have anything from scrambled egg flavor to liverwurst—"

"Oh," Danny said sarcastically. "Sounds great . . . liverwurst popcorn."

"Anyway," Sara continued. "It's really cool. We have to go there too."

"Okay, my love," Danny said. "We'll go there sometime this week also—ah-ha!" He pointed to a small sign along side the road. It read: WELCOME TO PROMISED LAND. "We made it, baby!"

"And in one piece!" Sara laughed. "Good job, honey, just keep going straight."

Another two miles passed and then the open country gave way to the town. To the left, streets could be seen with small houses and trailers spaced out on each side. But it was to the right that caught Sara's attention. "Look at this—it all used to be forest."

All the eye could see now was an empty field, with stumps and roots sticking up out of the ground. A few miles back, the forest regained its thickness as the incline to the mountain continued. "What a shame, the tornado really took its toll."

"That's quite a sight," agreed Danny.

Soon the empty field gave way to a lake with a small sandy beach. "You love the beach so much," Sara said. "There you go."

Danny looked over and grinned. "Yeah, but where's the boardwalk?"

"Actually, this is part of the State Park."

"Part of it? How big is the park?"

"About 3,000 acres, give or take," Sara answered.

"Wow, that's big."

"Yep. Did you know we are now 1,800 feet above sea level?"

Danny looked over at Sara and raised his eyebrows. "Really? Did you measure it?"

Sara laughed. "I'm filled with useless knowledge that my father has passed down to me. Look up here on the left. It's the main hangout, the B.Y.I."

A small bar with dark wood siding and white paint came into view. "*That's* the main hangout?" To Danny, it looked like a Swiss chalet.

"Absolutely," she replied. "The famous Barn Yard Inn. We'll probably have a couple meals there. They have really good food. Make your next left."

As Danny made the turn onto the street, the pavement changed to gravel. "Red streets?" Danny asked. "What are these roads made out of?"

"Red clay and stone actually," answered Sara.

"Oh," Danny said. To him, it looked like they were traveling up a river of blood. As they drove, he looked out his window at the houses they passed. "No signs of life yet."

"Doesn't surprise me," Sara said. "Like I said, most people will come up on the weekend. But there are still plenty of people around." As if on cue, they passed a house where a mother and father were playing with two little girls in their yard. "That's the Kinders," she said. "They're very nice. Make this sharp left here."

As he started to turn the corner, a kid on a four-wheeler shot past them. "Whoa!" Danny said, slamming on the brakes. The kid glanced at them quickly and kept on going. "That was close."

"Yeah, I should have warned you. A couple of streets over there's a family that have a couple of kids, each with their own four-wheeler."

"Oh."

"If you're a teenager and live here year round, it can sometimes get boring," Sara said.

"Don't they have Playstations up here?" Danny asked with a smile. His new wife forbade him to bring his own Playstation with them on their honeymoon.

"I guess not," Sara replied. "After this bend slow down, it's up here on the right."

"Finally," Danny said with an over exaggerated sigh. He rounded the bend and slowed the car down. "Where?"

"There!" Sara said, pointing up.

Up a rather steep incline sat the house. A boulder in front of the house had *The Evans* carved into it. The driveway was made out of stone with large rocks on either side. Danny started to guide the Intrepid up the steep driveway. About halfway up, the car stopped. He pressed lightly on the accelerator, only to have the car's tires spin in the gravel. "I have to back down and come up with a little more speed," Danny decided. He threw the gear into reverse and started to back down, careful to avoid the large rocks that outlined the driveway. Once down, he put the car in drive and came back up with more speed. Reaching the top this time, he saw a small area behind the boulder for parking. He pulled the car into the spot, put it in park and killed the ignition.

Unbuckling his seat belt, Danny leaned over and kissed his bride. "We're here."

"We're here," Sara repeated. "Happy honeymoon."

"Happy honeymoon to you," Danny said and kissed her again. This one held for some time. After releasing he said, "I love you."

"I love you too," she replied, her eyes watering. "Well," she said, wiping a tear from her cheek. "How about we start this honeymoon?"

"Absolutely," he said as they got out of the car and stretched.

"Hope you're ready for a good workout," Sara said.

"I'm ready!" Danny said, a little too anxious.

Sara smiled. "I was referring to lugging all of our stuff up that flight of stairs."

Danny looked up and saw stone steps with a wooden railing leading the way up a tall hill to the house, a yellow rancher with a large wooden deck made from southern yellow pine. "Oh."

As they started to unload their luggage, a voice called out from below them at street level. "Sara?"

The couple turned their attention toward the driveway. After a moment a young woman with short blonde hair came scuttling up. "I thought I saw a car come up here!"

"Hi, Anna," Sara said as she set down a suitcase and walked over to greet her. "How are you?"

"Oh, I'm fine. What are you—oh, who's this?" Anna asked, noticing Danny for the first time.

"Danny, come here," Sara called.

"Danny?" Anna whispered with a smile.

Danny closed the rear passenger door and walked over. "Anna, I would like for you to meet Danny Walker—my husband."

"Husband? Girl, I didn't know you got married! Oh wow, congratulations, let me see that ring!" Anna cried, grabbing Sara's hand. "Oh, that's beautiful." Turning her attention from Sara, Anna said, "Danny, it's nice to meet you."

"Likewise," he replied.

"Are you on your honeymoon?"

"Yes, we are," said Sara. "What brings you up here?"

"Oh, you know how it is with me, Sara. Daddy is away on another business trip and mother is throwing another boring cocktail party. So I asked for the keys to the house and here I am. Besides I have a date tomorrow night."

Sara raised her eyebrows. "Oh really? Who's the lucky guy?"

"Some guy I just met at the Canadensis gas station," Anna giggled. "He is gorgeous; a real hunk!" "Really? Well, good luck with him—"

"Thanks," Anna said. Then suddenly her face lit up, as if some important revelation just dawned on her. "We're having dinner at the B.Y.I. tomorrow night. Why don't you join us? Let's make it a double date! That would be great!"

"Uh, I don't know—" Danny started to say.

"Oh, come on!" Anna pleaded.

"Well, we'll see," Sara said. "We're not sure what we had planned yet—"

"Great!" Anna exclaimed. "Okay, I'll let you guys get back to unpacking. See you later!" And with that she hurried down the decline and out of view.

"Yeah, see you much, much later," Danny said into Sara's ear.

Sara laughed. "I'm sorry about that. Anna Morris lives on the next street over. You'd know which one; it's the nicest in Promised Land. Her father is some rich business tycoon or something so she comes up here a lot . . . and usually not alone."

"I see," Danny said. "Well, the gear is unpacked."

"Great! You ready?"

Danny smiled. "I was born ready." They both grabbed some luggage and headed up the steep stairway. To the left of them was the house but as they neared the top and the ground leveled out Sara directed his attention to the right.

"See that?" said Sara, pointing to an area of the small yard. A small circle made up of red bricks sat a few yards from a wooden swing. Inside the circle were the remains of burnt firewood. "That's our little campfire site. There are some lounge and folding chairs in the shed over there and at night we can roast marshmallows and make homemade smores."

"Cool, I've never made homemade smores before," Danny said.

"You haven't?" Sara asked, a little surprised.

"I mean I've had them before, you know, store bought," he said. "But I have never made my own before."

"Boy," Sara said. "You've got a lot to learn. I'll show you all kinds of cool stuff."

"I bet you will," Danny said with his one-track mind.

"Come on, Romeo," she replied. "I'll show you the house."

Three wooden steps took them to a tiny porch. Danny held open the screen door as Sara unlocked the front door. After a moment of fidgeting with the keys, the door swung inward. She was about to enter when Danny put a hand on her shoulder and halted her. "Allow me," he said. Placing the luggage down, he grabbed his bride and lifted her into his arms. Wrapped tightly together, they stepped over the threshold.

"Thank you, sweetie," Sara beamed. "That was nice."

"You're welcome," he replied as he turned and started to pick up the suitcases.

"Before you do that," Sara said, grabbing his arm. "Let me show you the house."

"Sure."

"Okay, um, we are now standing in the dining room," she said. Next to a window to their right was a table set. Sara leaned over the table and pulled up the blind, letting the sun shine brightly in. Against the far wall sat a small hutch and an additional chair. To the left was a small room. Danny peeked in to see a small bedroom.

"Hey, that's neat," Danny said, stepping inside. Between the bed and the small dresser, was what looked like a window. Pushing a small curtain aside, Danny poked his head into the living room. Glancing around, he saw a couple of recliners facing a small television.

"Hey, we'll get to that room in a minute," Sara said, pulling him back in. "A long time ago this used to be where the house ended. Then my grandfather decided to add on again and he built the living room. Come on."

Making a left out of the bedroom, they entered a hallway. Sara opened the first door on the left. "Here we have the bathroom. And down here we have the other two bedrooms." She opened the door to the right. "This will be ours; it's the biggest of the three." Inside was a queen-sized bed surrounded by a dresser and a nightstand. At the front of the room was a small closet to hang clothes in.

"Let's stop here," Danny said, grabbing Sara from behind and kissing her neck. She smiled and hooked her arm behind his head and turned slightly so they were face to face. She looked into his eyes and saw everything she had ever wanted to see when it came to the man of her dreams. Love, compassion, tenderness, but with an inner strength unlike she had ever known. He also provided for them with his landscaping job, allowing her to pursue her college degree to become a nurse. Best of all, she knew he loved her with all his heart and soul.

"Honey?" Sara said.

"Yes?"

"Do you know how happy you make me?"

Danny smiled, trying to hide his swelling tears. "Thank you, honey. Yesterday you made me the happiest man in the world."

She leaned up and kissed him deeply. When she finished she said, "Come on, let me show you the rest of the house. From the way you're looking at me, I doubt you'll see very much of the other rooms this week."

Danny laughed. "All right, lead the way."

To the right past the dining room was a cozy narrow kitchen, which housed a microwave and other small items. Although it was small, it consisted of everything they needed, including a washer and dryer, sink and refrigerator. At the end of the kitchen, Sara slid back a wooden sliding door. "This is the pantry." Danny took a step inside and saw a vacuum cleaner and a cabinet filled with food and other kitchen supplies.

"Last room," Sara said, leading him into the living room. This was the largest of the rooms. It consisted not only of the two recliners and television that Danny saw earlier, but a couch, an additional chair and a fireplace. Behind the couch was a waist-high bookshelf, extending the whole length of the room.

A sliding glass door led from the living room to the large deck, which held a picnic table and several chairs. "Wow," Danny said, leaning over the railing. "You can see half the town from here."

"Isn't it nice?"

"Very."

"And how about this air?" Sara asked, taking a deep breath.

Danny took a deep breath also. "Ah yes, it's um, air."

"It's so fresh and unpolluted. And it's so quiet here, I just love it up here," Sara said.

"I can certainly see why," said Danny.

Sara turned to him. "Danny, I just wanted to thank you."

Puzzled, Danny asked, "For what?"

"For allowing us to come here on our honeymoon," she answered.

"Are you kidding? This is great!"

"It really is," Sara commented. "But what I mean is that I know you really had your heart set on going somewhere tropical on our honeymoon like the Caribbean or somewhere like that. And I promise you someday we will go there. But to me, on this occasion, this is the best place we could have gone—"

"Honey don't be silly," Danny said, hugging her. "Believe me when I tell you, there is nowhere else on Earth I'd rather be."

"Good," Sara smiled. "Me too."

"Okay?"

Sara nodded. "I'm just glad we're together."

"Me too," Danny said. Then, his eyes narrowed. "What's that over there? A squirrel?"

Following his gaze over the railing, Sara spotted a small animal near their car. "Oh, that's a chipmunk."

"Oh."

"You've never seen a chipmunk before?" Sara asked, amused.

"Just Alvin, Simon and Theodore," Danny replied. "I even have their Christmas album!"

Sara giggled. "I take it then you've never seen one before." Danny nodded sheepishly. "Well, there's a ton of them up here," she said. "And bears too."

"Bears?"

"Oh, didn't I mention that this is bear country?"

"Um, no."

"Relax," Sara said. "Only black bears live around here. Half the town feed them scraps all the time. We sometimes leave bread out for them."

"They come right into the yard?" Danny asked.

"Oh yeah," Sara said. "We look out the kitchen window and watch them."

"Oh, that's cool," he said.

"Well, what do you want to do first?" Sara asked.

Danny motioned back toward the house. "Oh, you know what I want to do."

"Okay, what do you want to do second?" Sara asked again.

"I don't know," Danny replied. "I'll follow your lead, it's up to you."

"Okay, would you like to go for a little walk up town?"

"Up town? Sure. And do what?"

"Just look around. I want to check out where the tornado hit."

"Okay."

"You sure?"

"Yes, I'm sure. I've got all night to ravish you," Danny smiled.

"Okay, great. Let's get unpacked and turn everything on and then we'll head out."

"Sounds like a plan."

Walking back into the kitchen, Sara paused by the dryer and reached above it to the fuse box. Leaning on the dryer, she opened the box and started reading the small tabs that told her which switches to turn on. After a moment she flicked on the appropriate switches. "There," she said. "Now for the water."

"Water?"

"Yeah, you know the wet stuff?"

"Ha, ha" Danny said. "I know what water is but how do we turn it on?"

"We don't." She smiled. "You do."

"Huh?"

"Follow me," she said and they went out the front door. Instead of walking down the stairway they went straight past the small campfire site. "Over here is the well." A few yards away was what looked to Danny like a doghouse. There was a small entrance surrounded by an A-framed roof. "My grandfather built this too."

"Really? Your grandfather was quite a guy, huh?" Danny asked.

"Yes. Yes, he was," Sara said, a hint of sadness in her voice.

"I wish I could have met him."

"Yeah," she replied. "Me too."

Stooping inside, Danny saw an extremely old ladder leading down into what he conceived as a pit. "Spooky."

"It leads to the well," Sara said. "Just climb down to the bottom and you'll see a holding tank and a pump. I've already turned on the electricity but you still need to turn the valve on to release the water."

"How far down does it go?"

"The actual well is a hundred and eighty-five feet deep. But years ago my grandfather and my father built a cement footer over top the well so now it's only about fifteen feet. Think you can handle that?"

"Of course, I can handle anything, baby," Danny said in his most macho tone of voice. He turned and, kneeling down, swung himself onto the ladder. After the first rung the old ladder let out a terrible creak. "Um," Danny said, looking up into the sunlight. "Is this thing gonna hold me?"

"Of course," came the reply from just outside the entrance.

"Okay," he sighed and continued down. As he climbed down Danny noticed that the walls were made out of cinderblock. He could only imagine the work that Sara's family put into this structure. Reaching the cemented bottom, Danny was in an area that was no more than eight-foot square. He turned to his left and saw the holding tank and pump. There was enough sunlight finding its way down that Danny easily spotted the valve attached to the pump. "Let's see," he mumbled. "Righty-tighty so lefty is loosey." Having said that, he turned the valve to the left. The valve squealed, but turned. Danny heard a very low rumble and knew that the water had been released. "Piece of cake," he smirked and headed back up.

"Okay," he said as he reached the top. "Mission accomplished—" He stopped short—she was nowhere in sight. He climbed the rest of the way out and stooped to get through the low entrance way. "Sara?" All was quiet. He walked slowly back toward the house. Then something to his right caught his attention. The shed door was open, swaying slightly from the light breeze. He walked over to the door and flung it the rest of the way open. "Hey, Sara—" Inside on one side were lounge chairs, fishing poles, nets and other items. On the other side there was a wooden workbench, saws, hammers and other useful tools—but no Sara. He backed out of the shed and was beginning to close the door when something suddenly grabbed him. "Ah!" Danny yelped.

"Whoa," Sara said. "Did I scare you?"

Trying to recover, Danny snorted. "Of course not. I was just wondering where you ran off to."

"Sorry about that. I went inside and got the key to the shed. I wanted to see if all the chairs and stuff were still there. Then I went to check on you but I went around the other side of the shed; we probably walked right by each other."

"Oh. So, is everything cool?"

"Yep, everything is just how it was last time I was here," she replied. "How'd you make out? I see you didn't drown yourself."

"I knew what I was doing," Danny retorted, sticking out his chest. "You probably don't know it yet, but I'm quite the handyman."

"Really?" Sara laughed. "Well, that's good to know."

"You better believe it, I'm the Tim "The Tool Man" Taylor of South Jersey!"

Sara laughed again. In reality, Sara knew that Danny was not much of a handyman. After his parents divorced, he went to live with his mother. When she remarried, Danny refused to get close to his stepfather, even though the man had done nothing to him. So for most of his adolescence, he kept to himself and didn't learn how to do anything except how to get into trouble. The way Danny and his stepfather get along now, Sara would have never suspected that there had been any problems in his childhood.

"Hey," she said. "You wouldn't mind if we unpacked later tonight, would you?"

"Mind? I don't care if we never unpack!"

"Good. We'll do that then. I just want to get this walk in before we lose the daylight."

"That's fine with me," he said.

"Good. Let me go lock up the house and we'll go."

"Lock up the house? You have burglars up here?"

"Not that I know of. I guess it's just old habit," she said and hurried to the house. "Besides," she said a moment later. "You never know."

"That's true," Danny agreed. "Ready? Let's walk."

After descending the stairway, they started down the steep driveway, the momentum making them stride faster. Sara laughed as Danny tried to maintain his footing.

Once they reached the road, they headed left. As they walked, Danny looked at each house they passed by, all of them lifeless and dark. Sensing her husband's thoughts, Sara grabbed his hand. "Wait until Labor Day, it will be the complete opposite. There will be constant noise, traffic jams—it will be crazy."

"I don't know if I'd like that more or not," Danny said. "It's nice now."

They continued on through several streets. As they started down the last one that led to the main road, Danny became aware of crunching sounds behind him. Turning back, he saw a blue mini van coming slowly towards them, the tires crunching on the clay and stone road. When the vehicle reached them, it slowed and then stopped. A lady with short brown hair rolled down the passenger window. "Hi, Sara!"

"Hi, Mrs. Kinder, Mr. Kinder, how are you?"

"We're doing just fine," Mr. Kinder said from the driver's side. "Say hello to Sara, girls."

"Hi, Sara!" came the reply from the two young girls in the back seat.

"Hi, Stacy, hi, Lisa," Sara said.

"Who is this nice young man with you?" Mrs. Kinder asked with a smile.

"Mr. and Mrs. Kinder, I would like you to meet Danny Walker," Sara beamed. "My husband."

"Husband? Oh, congratulations, sweetie!" Mrs. Kinder exclaimed, reaching out the window to give Sara a quick hug. "When did you get married?"

"Yesterday," Sara replied.

"Oh wow," Mrs. Kinder said. "I bet your mother was a mess, wasn't she?"

"Yes, she was," Sara laughed. "I was doing fine until I took a peek at her. When I saw her crying, I started crying."

"Danny, it's nice to meet you," Mr. Kinder piped in.

"The pleasure is mine," Danny said.

"Sara Evans married," Mrs. Kinder continued. "Well, God bless you both. Danny, you take care of her."

"I will," Danny said.

"So where are you guys off to?" Sara asked.

"We're going into Canadensis to get the kids some candy," Mr. Kinder answered.

"Well, have fun, girls," Sara said, waving at Stacy and Lisa.

"We will," the young girls said in unison.

"Take care you two and congratulations once again," Mrs. Kinder said.

"Thank you," Sara and Danny both said as the family drove away.

"Wow," Danny grinned. "Actual people."

"Oh, stop it," Sara laughed as they continued their route to the main road.

Chapter Four

Henry Watson walked clumsily up the old dirt trail. He often took one of the many mountain trails to get away from town for a while. There usually wasn't anybody around this far up the mountain, even during the busy times. He would have preferred to hang out with his best friend George Stine, but George wasn't around. He stopped on occasion to take a bottle of whiskey out of his pocket. He stared at the alcohol in his hands for some time with great lust, before finally taking a tremendous gulp. Sighing with great satisfaction, he continued on.

As he walked, Henry's mind wandered back to this time last year. His wife, Melinda, had filed for divorce, accused him of being an alcoholic. That always made Henry laugh. He wasn't an alcoholic, no way. He just liked to have a drink now and again, that's all. She always said he never wanted to spend any time with her or their daughter, Rebecca. But, Henry smiled, she did have one good idea. She told him that since he loved coming up to the mountains with his friends and getting drunk all the time, why don't he just move up there permanently? *That was the smartest thing to ever come out of that wench's mouth*, he thought sourly.

Now, he had the life. He owned his very own trailer in Promised Land, a steady job in Allentown and all the whiskey he wanted. On the weekends, some of Henry's old friends still come up and complain about their wives. *Well not me,* Henry thought, *I'm free. Free at last.* He walked a little farther, then stopped, digging hastily into his pocket for another swig of that liquid freedom. He chugged long and hard on the beverage, trying to clear his mind of thoughts of Melinda, the evil witch.

He smiled and swallowed the last drop of his whiskey. Henry's eyes closed as he savored the taste. As he began to lower the bottle, Henry opened his eyes and stopped short. Ahead of him and to the left, was a huge hole in the mountainside. Along side of the hole, were several trees lying on their side. To Henry, the stumps that remained looked like giant toothpicks. Turning further to his left he noticed a small path of damaged trees. "The tornado must have just nipped this spot," Henry said out loud. Soon he turned his attention back to the gaping hole in the mountain. Looking at all the fresh debris that laid around the opening, Henry wondered if the tornado had reopened up a cave from long ago or had simply made a new one. He peered into the hole, into the darkness. Then he turned and, shading his eyes, looked up at the blazing hot sun. Glancing back toward the cave, he shrugged and entered in.

Chapter Five

Tom Reimer had almost finished wiping down the bar when Joanne Simpson came in. When the door opened, it triggered a small bell above to chime. "Hi, Joanne," Tom smiled as he continued to wipe. "How was your night?"

The slender woman with curly brown hair took a seat on one of the barstools. "It was exciting. I watched Jay Leno and went to sleep. How about you?"

"Same old, same old," he replied. "Oh, the steak guy called and said he would be here the day after next."

"That's fine," she said. "It won't be busy again for another week, we won't run out before then."

Joanne's father owned and ran The Barn Yard Inn ever since she was a little girl. Two years ago this winter, he signed the restaurant over to her. Since then, she has run the place quite well, making customers just as happy. Her father was a well-respected man and she wanted to earn that same respect from the people.

They moved here when she was twelve, shortly after her mother, Maria, died in a car accident. When Joanne was very young, they would come here on vacation, escaping city life for a while. It was Maria's favorite place in the whole world and it's where they had most of their fondest memories. That's why after she died Joanne's father decided to move them to Promised Land. He always said he felt closer to her mother here, like she was still with them in some way.

"I know what you mean," Tom said, interrupting her thoughts. "It's been slow lately."

"You haven't been around long enough to know just how slow it can get," Joanne said. "After September, it's absolutely dead. How about old Henry, has he been in yet?"

"Of course," Tom said. "Bought himself some Wild Turkey. That usually only lasts a couple of hours, though. I'm surprised he hasn't come back yet."

"Yeah," Joanne smirked. "He's our main source of income in the off season."

"Hey," Tom said, glancing out the side window. "Who's that?"

"Potential customers, I hope," Joanne joked as she turned and looked.

Walking hand in hand down the street was a young couple. Joanne stood up and walked over to the window. Tom followed behind her, dish towel still in hand.

"Oh," she said. "That's Sara Evans; Mark and Cindy's daughter."

"Okay," Tom said as he flung the towel over his shoulder. "Who's the guy?"

"I don't know," she replied. "Obviously her boyfriend. That's good, Sara's a nice girl."

"You know her well?"

"I watched her grow up," Joanne said.

"Oh," Tom said. As Joanne had mentioned a moment ago, Tom hadn't been in Promised Land very long, only a couple of months. He was born and raised in Allentown and had been a resident there most of his life.

Last year when he was laid off from his job of ten years as a factory foreman, he decided it was time to relocate. Almost every company in the city was cutting back due to the economy. Being somewhat of a political expert, Tom didn't think that the economy was as bad as everybody said it was. But if not, why were companies either going under or severely cutting their staff?

Executives of big corporations think this way: why pay two people to do a job when you can pay one and just work him to death?

Tom's final effort before deciding to move was to apply at the one corporation that seemed to be thriving amongst all the other decaying companies. It was a pharmaceutical company called Intech. But he was told that they had all the staff that they could handle. Disappointed, he looked around a little while longer then decided it was time to make a change in his life.

He decided to take time and explore the state. He wanted to find the ideal place to live, to start over, maybe even meet someone nice and start a family.

The first time he laid eyes on Promised Land, he fell in love with it. It was not too far from his hometown, but far enough away at the same time. It was perfect—except that there were no job opportunities. After deciding that this was where he wanted to live, Tom began to inquire in town if there was any work to be found. Everybody he talked to was very nice, but also very unhelpful. No one knew of any jobs available.

He had just begun to run out of hope when he met Joanne Simpson. It was the busy season and she was short handed, so she had agreed to temporarily bring him on board. As luck would have it, her full time bartender was moving across the country to Oregon, to be closer with his family. Tom had no real bartending experience before, but Joanne trained him and now he enjoys serving the residents of Promised Land.

He didn't have a place to live yet when he had first decided to move, so Joanne allowed him to stay in a room above her garage for a month until he found his own house to rent. Although he had not known her long and she was thirteen years his elder, Tom had grown very fond of Joanne Simpson. He promised himself that someday he would gather up the courage to ask her to go on a date. But as for now he was happy with where he was and what he was doing. "You really do know everybody, don't you?"

Remembering all the years she had been in Promised Land, Joanne smiled. "I guess I do."

Chapter Six

Danny and Sara stopped at the main road. To the left of them was the Barn Yard Inn and to the right was another small street leading them back the way they came. Across the main road was a sidewalk followed by a split-log fence. This continued further down until the beginning of the State Park, where the lake was. They could see the flat land made barren by the tornado. "See that," Sara said, pointing across the street to a small gravel trail that started where the fence ended.

"Where?" Danny asked, following her direction. "Oh, the trail?"

"Yeah," she replied. "That's the beginning of one of the hundred different hiking trails around here and that's where we're going."

For the first mile or so, the trail was very barren. Where once a lush forest existed, now was the home of emptiness. There were, however, reminders left behind of what used to be. Hundreds of stumps were there, protruding from the ground like giant wooden stakes awaiting a mammoth vampire. There were still some trees there, lying on their sides in massive stacks, awaiting departure. A few squirrels ran about, frantically looking for food. It was quite a sight to see.

"Wow," Danny said, amazed by the view. "That tornado sure did a number on this place."

"Told ya," Sara said as they continued along the gravel trail. "Some of the trees destroyed here were well over a hundred years old."

After walking for quite some time, the trees started to thicken and the forest began to take form again. They came to a fork in the trail and Sara led them up the left one. "This is a wilderness trail," she said. "A lot of hikers come up here."

"How far up does it go?"

"I'm not sure. There are over fifty miles of trails throughout this part of the mountain. I'm not sure how far they actually go, I don't know if anybody knows that. A lot of the mountain is relatively untouched."

Danny looked up toward the sky. "Wow, we've lost track of time here. It's starting to get dark already."

Sara also looked up. A purple haze began to stretch across the sky. "Well, time flies when you're having fun. The next trail coming up will take us back toward town."

Chapter Seven

As his eyes became accustomed to the darkness, Henry started to get a feeling of his surroundings. He was in a cavern and he could hear water dripping from somewhere high above him. Using the cave wall as a guide, he walked farther back. It seemed to Henry to go on for some time. After a while he came upon what looked to be an entrance to another section of the cavern. He continued on.

The second cavern, Henry discovered, was much larger than the first. As he walked he had the feeling that the farther he went, the wider the cavern grew. After a few more steps, his foot struck something, causing him to stumble.

"Ouch," he grunted, as he squatted down to see what he hit.

Grabbing a lighter from his breast pocket, the gray bearded man flicked it on. From what he could tell, it was the skeleton of a small animal, maybe a rabbit. "Hmm," he mumbled. "That's strange."

Standing back up, he continued farther into the cave. When he first entered, he could still see fairly well because the sun was filtering in. But now, he saw no traces of the sun any more and he realized that more time had elapsed than he had originally thought. He was just about to turn and find his way out when he struck something much larger. Henry's arms flailed as he tried to regain his footing, but found nothing to grab onto. He fell and landed hard, knocking the wind out of himself.

Chapter Eight

"Yes," Allan Parker said into the telephone receiver. "Thank you. You too, bye-bye." As he hung up the phone, he heard Bill Darley's truck pull up outside. A moment later, Bill was standing in front of Allan.

"I expected you back a lot sooner," Allan said, standing up. "You were supposed to have the rest of the day off but now the day is almost over."

Bill's usual happy-go-lucky face was rock solid. "Allan?"

"Yes?" Allan asked.

"We found another one," he replied.

"Another deer? I was afraid of that. I think I'm gonna have to close some of the trails in the mountain until we figure out what is going on around here. We'll post signs everywhere—"

"Allan?"

"Yes," Allan said.

"This one wasn't a deer."

Allan's heart jumped a beat. "Wasn't a deer? Then what was it?"

"Follow me," Bill said as he turned and left the ranger's office. Allan followed him outside to Bill's blue pick up truck. "I had to go get Charlie to help me with this."

"Charlie? Charlie doesn't work for me, he's just your friend," Allan said. "You know the rules."

"Yeah, I know the rules," Bill said, obviously shaken. "But this was an unusual circumstance."

"How unusual?"

"This unusual," Bill said as he lowered the tailgate and stepped aside.

Allan walked up to the rear of the truck and looked inside. "What the—" For a split second, he thought his eyes were playing a trick on him.

Inside the truck, was the mangled body of an adult black bear.

Chapter Nine

The light was quickly fading as the newly married couple made their way back down the dirt trail toward town. On this particular trail, the damage was less severe and the forest was thick. "Isn't this nice?" Sara asked. "It's so peaceful."

"It is," Danny agreed. "It almost seems like another world. I've never been someplace before where it was so . . . quiet."

"Yeah," she smiled.

"I mean, all day today, I didn't really hear anything," Danny said. "No rabbits hopping or squirrels running—"

"Are you sure?"

"No, not really," Danny admitted. "Maybe I just wasn't paying attention."

"Yeah," Sara said. "Personally, I was too overwhelmed with the sights."

"Yeah, I know what you mean," Danny agreed.

"I can picture us fifty years from now walking down the same old trail," Sara said, smiling.

"I can't picture us walking another fifty minutes—my feet are killing me!" Danny exclaimed. "How about giving me a piggy-back ride the rest of the way into town?"

"I could," Sara laughed.

"You could not," Danny snorted. "I'm too heavy."

"Hey, I'm strong—see," Sara said, pausing to make a muscle. "Hop on."

"No way, I'll break your back," Danny replied. "I'm a hundred and eighty-five pounds, you know."

"I know and you will not break my back," she said. "Now come on, hop on."

"Okay," Danny sighed. "But when your back breaks, don't come crying to me!" Sara bent slightly over, preparing for the extra weight. He walked over to her. "You ready?"

"I was born ready," she said, trying to imitate him.

"Are you sure?"

"Come on already!"

"Okay, I warned you," Danny said and hopped onto her back. Sara's legs buckled under the additional weight, but then she straightened herself out. Danny crossed his arms in front of her.

"See?" Sara said. "I told you I could do it."

"Yeah," Danny said. "You're pretty strong. Now let's see you take a step or two."

"Fine," Sara scoffed and took a step forward. Then, another. She had walked several yards when her hands began to slip and she lost her grip on Danny's legs.

"Oh no!" Danny cried as he and Sara tumbled to the ground. Laughing, he asked, "Are you okay?"

Shaking with laughter, Sara held up her index finger. After a few moments she replied, "Oops—yes, I'm fine. Well, that was fun."

"Yeah, I'm impressed," he smiled. "That was a good show of strength."

"See?" Sara giggled. As she started to stand up, she turned her head slightly. Suddenly her giggle became a scream.

Chapter Ten

Henry tried to breathe, but gasped heavily instead. He struggled up to his knees. He then pounded on his chest, causing himself to cough. Slowly Henry stood up, taking several deep breaths as he tried to regulate his breathing. But as he did so, an awful coppery smell hit him hard, making him gag even more.

"What's that smell?" Henry croaked. He reached his hand inside his pocket to find it empty. "Where's my lighter?" He dropped to his knees again and started feeling around the rocky ground. After a moment, he found it.

Still on his knees, he lit it and shined the lighter in the direction from which he fell . . . and screamed.

Against the wall, maybe five feet tall, was a hill of bodies. From what he could tell, they were all animals. Limbs were strewn everywhere, literally covering this section of the cave's floor. He could make out several deer, raccoons, skunks and several other small animals. Countless marble eyes stared back at him, reflecting off the dim light.

Then he turned to his left. Henry's mouth opened and closed several times, but no sound emerged. Next to the large mound of animal bodies was a smaller hill. This one was human.

The light shone clearly on four bodies, the faces all distorted with terror. Henry took a step closer. Each victim appeared to be dressed identically. They were all wearing a blue and silver outfit with the word *Intech* in the upper right corner of each shirt. Then the lighter went out.

He flicked the device several times, but to no avail. "Come on!" he hissed. Henry turned and reached out with his arms, trying to find the cavern wall. He took several steps one way and then the other. He had totally lost his sense of direction. "I can't see! Which way is out?" He cried as he stumbled over another body. "What did this?"

Outside the cave entrance, the sun was fading fast and darkness was taking over.

Chapter Eleven

After a long moment of silence, Bill Darley asked, "What do you think?"

"What do I think?" Allan repeated. "I think we've got a serious problem. What around here can do this to a bear?"

"Maybe another bear?"

"No. No way. This is a full grown male, Bill. This thing weighed about four or five hundred pounds—"

"I know," Bill cut in. "If it weren't in so many pieces we wouldn't have been able to get it on the truck."

"Bill?"

"Yes?"

"We need to keep this between us for now, okay?"

"Okay, sure," said Bill. "And Charlie. He was there too."

"Yes. Please tell Charlie to keep his mouth shut about this too. I don't want to start a panic and have a dozen gun-toting guys running around in the woods," Allan said. "But I am going to close the trails starting tomorrow morning. I don't want anybody going into the mountain until we figure out what's going on."

"No problem, boss. I still think you should check that zoo and see if anything escaped."

"I already did," Allan said.

Bill smiled. "You did?"

"Well I ran out of ideas, so I tried yours," Allan said.

"And?"

"And nothing has escaped. They've never even had a grizzly on display before. The guy I talked to probably thinks I'm a real nut. Anyway, was there anything else?"

"One other thing."

"What?"

"We ran into George Stine earlier in the park," Bill replied.

"And?"

"And he was looking for his old buddy Henry. Says he disappeared."

"Well, Henry has a habit of doing that all the time," Allan said.

"That's what I told him," Bill said, pausing for a moment. "Hey, you don't think that, well, you know . . ."

"What?"

"That well maybe Henry . . ." Bill said, gesturing toward the dead bear.

"That Henry what? Spit it out! You think Henry ate the bear? What?" Allan asked, slightly annoyed.

"No. Do you think Henry met up with whatever did this?" Bill asked.

"No," Allan said right away. "I think Henry is drunk somewhere and is sleeping it off. This is what I'm talking about. I don't need wild rumors flying around."

"I won't say anything," Bill said. "Besides, tomorrow me and Charlie are going hunting up there to see if we can find whatever this thing is—"

"Oh, no you are not," Allan said. "I don't know how this happened but I'm sure we'll find the answer soon. I don't need you and Charlie up there shooting things up. Okay?"

"Okay," Bill said, disappointed.

"Good," Allan said, cooling down. "Listen, take care of this for me and then you're free to go."

"Okay," Bill replied again as he turned to leave. "Will do."

"And, Bill?" Allan said, stopping him.

"Yeah?"

"Be careful out there, okay?"

Bill smiled. "I will, Allan. Remember, I've got Old Betsy with me at all times."

"Good," Allan smiled back. "Go on, get outta here."

And with that, Bill jumped into his truck and sped off. Allan stayed outside for just a moment longer, studying the forest that lay across the road from the ranger station. Then, he turned and went inside.

Chapter Twelve

"What's wrong?" Danny asked, jumping to his feet.

"Look," Sara said as she stood up and pointed.

Danny walked over to his wife, looked down and said, "Whoa."

A yard in front of them, were the remains of what appeared to be a deer. It was hard to tell, for it was badly mangled. The entire torso was shredded, leaving most of the internal organs smeared on the ground. Danny also noticed that the throat had been torn out.

"What could have done that?" Danny asked.

"I don't know," Sara said. "I turned my head and there I was, nose to nose with it."

"Where *is* its nose?" Danny asked.

Several branches snapped to their left, and some trees started to rustle. "Okay," Danny said, lowering his voice. "Let's get back to town."

As they continued down the path, the last of the sunlight disappeared.

Chapter Thirteen

Henry Watson swung his arms from one side to the other, in the hopes of finding the cavern wall. He continued on, slowly placing each foot down, being careful to avoid the dead obstacles.

He was trying to decide which way to go next when he suddenly stopped. He listened intensely. There it was again. A small noise could be heard. It was a scraping noise. As he listened, the tiny hairs on the back of his neck stood up straight. The scraping noises were getting louder, closer. Henry had the sudden urge to flee but found he couldn't move. Then, there was another sound—a sick, slithering sound. Then it happened again. The third time it happened Henry recognized what it was: *The sound of small dead animals being kicked out of the way.* There was the same sound again, this time directly behind him. Henry's legs suddenly sprang to life and before he even knew it, he was running.

Chapter Fourteen

"Whew, what a walk," Danny said, taking a sip of water. He looked across the dining room table at Sara, who was staring off into space. "You okay?"

Sara blinked and looked back at Danny. "Yes, I'm fine."

"Really?"

"Really. I'm sorry, I guess that deer spooked me a little," Sara replied.

"It did get kind of spooky out there once it started getting dark," agreed Danny. "Do you think a bear did it?"

"No," answered Sara. "A bear only attacks if it is provoked or if its litter is threatened. A deer wouldn't do either one. Did you see the throat?"

"Yeah, I did," Danny replied. Then he tried to change the subject. "Anyway, did you have an overall nice day?"

Sara smiled. "I had an overall wonderful day."

"Good," Danny said, looking down at the table. "Do you know it is now our official honeymoon night?"

"Yes, it is," she said.

Danny smiled and his face reddened. Sara found this adorable. He looked up and stared at her with obvious bedroom eyes. For the first time today, he was at a loss for words.

"Do you want to go act like honeymooners?" Sara asked.

Danny smiled and nodded. Then he stood up and walking around the table, bent down and lifted his bride out of her seat. Forgetting about the deer and everything else in the world, he carried her down the hallway.

Chapter Fifteen

Henry pounded his way forward, not knowing where he was going or what was behind him. He ran fast. Faster than he had ever ran before. Faster than when he was a bright and promising student on his high school track team. He ran fast . . . Full speed into the cavern wall. He finally found the cavern wall. The impact knocked him to the ground. Dazed, he quickly stood up. He could feel warm liquid flowing freely from his temple and as he went to feel his head, he was suddenly pushed back against the wall with tremendous force.

Then, the floor disappeared from under his feet. No, the floor wasn't falling—*he was rising*. This realization suddenly hit Henry, and his last breath was used to scream.

Part Two

Confrontation
August 22nd

Chapter Sixteen

Sunlight shone through the partially opened blinds and onto Danny Walker's face. Squinting, he looked to his right and found that the other half of the bed was empty. The alarm clock on the nightstand read 11:45 AM. As he stretched and yawned loudly, an aroma hit him that made his mouth water. Quickly climbing out of bed, his hair a mess and dressed only in boxers, he headed toward the kitchen.

As he entered the dining room and turned the corner, he spotted the source of the wonderful smell. Already fully dressed, Sara stood in front of the stove, cooking fried eggs and bacon. He walked up behind her and gave her a hug. "Good morning."

"Good morning, love," she replied as she turned and kissed him. "Sleep well?"

"Obviously, it's almost noon."

"Well you were really tired honey and it is your vacation, you're allowed to sleep in." Sara took a step back and examined her new husband from head to toe. "You look attractive."

"I know," he joked.

"Listen, after your brunch I need you to do me a favor."

"Again?" Danny smiled.

"Anyways," she said, "A little ways past the B.Y.I. is the Mountain Market."

"The Mountain Market? What do they sell?"

"Everything. It's half a grocery store and deli and the other half is a hunting and live bait shop."

"A good combination," he said.

Sara laughed. "I need you to run there for me and pick up a few things."

"Sure. What do we need?"

"Milk and some other stuff for dinner later," she replied.

"We're not having live bait for dinner, are we?" Danny asked.

"Oh brother," Sara sighed.

*   *   *

The Intrepid reached the main road and turned left toward the Mountain Market. As he drove, Danny had several thoughts flow through his mind. The first and foremost was that he was now a married man. He kept glancing down at his wedding band and still awaited the reality of it all to hit him.

He thought back to what Sara had said yesterday, about what they would be like in fifty years. He couldn't even picture what life would be like in ten years, not alone fifty. Would they have children? Would they be as happy then as they were now? Danny was confident that life would only get better as the years passed by and that they wouldn't end up a statistic, like so many other previously married couples; like *his* parents. No, that would never happen. He and Sara were made for each other. He knew that the first time he ever laid eyes on her.

Once an aspiring actor, Danny did a lot of plays with several South Jersey theatre groups. In one particular play, he remembered the first night of dress rehearsal. He had walked down a flight of stairs that led to the dressing rooms below the stage. Attached to several doors were the names of all the actors in the play. Whichever door your name was on, that was where your costume was and where your make-up would be applied.

Danny reached his door and, as he entered, came face to face with an angel. She was sitting toward him, applying the last bit of mascara to another actor. He remembered stopping in the doorway, just staring at her.

She looked up at him, with a quizzical look on her face. "Are you lost?" She had asked.

"No, no, I'm right where I need to be," he had managed to mumble.

"Okay, have a seat, I'll be right with you."

"Take your time," Danny replied and took a seat in front of a large mirror encircled by lights.

After a few moments, the dream girl had finished with the other guy and approached him. "I don't put make-up on complete strangers," she said as she extended her hand. "I'm Sara Evans."

Danny reached up and shook her hand. What beautiful blue eyes, he remembered thinking. "And you are?" Sara said after several moments.

"Oh, ah, Danny. Danny Walker," he stuttered, still shaking her hand.

"It's nice to meet you, Danny Walker," she replied with a smile. "If I am to do your make-up, I'm going to need my hand back."

"Oh," Danny smiled, quickly letting go. "Sorry."

He remembered how warmly she had smiled back at him. And it was then that he knew he had found the girl he was going to marry. Danny had never believed in love at first sight before that moment. But as he sat there, having blush applied to his cheeks, he didn't doubt for one moment that he was in love with the girl.

It wasn't until after the performance that he had gathered up the courage to ask her out. He can remember how fast she had replied. "Great," was the answer with no hesitation. Was it love at first sight for her too? Danny often wondered but had never asked Sara that question before.

Returning to the present, Danny looked to his left and saw the B.Y.I. Only one car was in the parking lot thus far. Continuing farther up the road, he also passed two churches and a miniature golf course.

The second thought Danny was dwelling on was Promised Land. It seemed so picturesque, so peaceful, that Danny had surprisingly already taken a strong liking to it. Everything seemed so perfect, maybe too perfect, if there was such a thing.

Then up on the left Danny saw the Mountain Market. The outside of the building was painted in a faded light blue. There was no room to park at the store but there was a dirt parking lot across the street. Danny turned into the lot and parked the car. The final thought Danny briefly had as he crossed the empty street was that of the mangled deer they had stumbled upon yesterday.

Chapter Seventeen

Allan Parker stared at the map of Promised Land that was stapled to the bulletin board on the far wall of the station. Where the six deer and the bear had been found, Allan placed red tacks. He studied the marks carefully, studying the pattern. The first body was found on the highest hiking trail that the mountain had. Beyond that, who knew how many might be dead.

The second was found ten miles further south, on a well-traveled wilderness path. The third, a little further down than the second. To Allan, the killings were in only one pattern: *they were heading straight down the mountain toward the town.* Allan started to get a very bad feeling in his stomach when the screen door slammed shut, making him jump. Allan turned to see the grinning face of George Stine.

"What's the matter, Allan, jumpy?" George asked.

"No," Allan replied. "I was just concentrating on something. What can I do for you?"

"Henry Watson is missing," George said, the smile vanishing from his face. "I want you to find him."

"George, you know as well as I do that Henry has a bad habit of doing this time and time again," Allan said. "Did you try his house?"

"Do you think I would come calling on you if Henry was home?" George said angrily. "I tell you he's missing."

"Is his car in the driveway?"

"Yeah."

"Okay, so he's either sleeping and didn't hear you or he's drunk somewhere—"

"We need to put together a search party—"

"Whoa," Allan said. Then glancing at the bulletin board and all those red tacks, he sighed. "Tell you what, George, I'll search the town for Henry. If I don't find him, I'll check some of his favorite hangouts in the mountain. He's bound to be in one of those places. Okay?"

George hesitated for a moment, and then nodded. "I want to go with you."

"That's really not necessary," Allan replied. "Just go on home and I'll call you with any information."

"Let me ask you a question, Allan."

"Sure."

"Why is that no-brain deputy of yours out posting signs that the trails are closed?" George asked. "Are you hiding something from us?"

"No, George, I'm not hiding anything," Allan said. "We've had a small problem with some of the wildlife lately and we're just looking into it, that's all."

"What sort of problem?"

"It's nothing to be concerned about, George," Allan said, not sure if he was lying or not. "We've had a couple of dead deer, that's all. We'll take care of it."

"If there's a problem you owe it to the people of this town to inform them of any—"

"George," Allan said sternly. "I said we'd handle it. Now go home."

"All right, Allan," George said, heading toward the door. "But I'm warning you, I want updates every hour—"

"Okay."

"Something fishy going on here—"

"Good-bye, George."

Allan slumped into his chair and put his head in his hands. He could have told George about the dead bear but then George would have told everybody in town and then the panic would have erupted, creating an even worse situation. Allan opened his desk drawer and took out a .45 pistol. He released the clip, made sure it was loaded and then slammed it home again. He grabbed his keys and, glancing one last time at the map, left the office.

Chapter Eighteen

Danny stared quizzically at the empty fish tank in front of him and wondered what type of fish it once held. He was in the hunting section of the store, which consisted of nets, fishing poles, tents and other useful equipment. After looking around for another minute, he reentered the first part of the store, the grocery part.

He walked up and down the aisles, looking first at the shelves and then down at the list Sara had made for him. He had just spotted the first item on the list when someone called out his name. Danny recognized the voice and winced. Turning around, he said, "Oh, hi, Anna."

"Hi back," Anna Morris laughed. "Whatcha doing?"

"Just a little shopping," he replied.

"Cool. So, how do you like our little town?"

"Actually, I like it very much," Danny said. "It's nice and quiet up here."

"Yeah," Anna sighed. "A little too quiet for my taste." Growing up in a family where being loved meant you were given money and freedom, Anna has had more than her share of nights that were anything but quiet. Back home she had more friends than she cared to count, some because they genuinely liked her but most because of her money.

Unlike her parents, Anna never was able to grasp the fun in sitting at cocktail parties while everybody talked about their investments, the Dow Jones or politics. Anna didn't know or care what the Dow Jones was and why everybody talked about it. She just liked to have fun. And since she was never gracious enough to attend one of her mother's gatherings, she'd always come up here with a group of friends and party. This week, however, her friends were busy so she decided to come up and make new friends if at all possible. It never took Anna long to get a date. She was rich and attractive, and wasn't shy about either. "So, are we still on for tonight?"

"Tonight?"

"Yeah, silly, remember yesterday? You, Sara, me and my hunk all going to the B.Y.I. for dinner?"

"Oh, I didn't know that was set in stone—"

"Of course, it was! It'll be a blast, you wait and see. Tell Sara we'll meet you guys there at seven, bye!"

Danny just stood there in the aisle, holding a jar of mayonnaise. "What just happened here?" he asked out loud. The jar didn't answer.

Chapter Nineteen

Sara finished drying the last of the breakfast dishes and walked out onto the deck. She loved it out there. The view was breathtaking, the air smelled clean and the sun was warm.

Across town and just above the trees, she could see the cross on top of the Baptist church's steeple. Sara always felt a certain calmness when she looked at it. It reminded her of her deep-rooted belief in Christianity that she grew up with. Whether it was just the sun reflecting off the cross or her eyes playing tricks on her she wasn't sure, but every time she stared at that beautiful symbol, it always seemed to glow.

The familiar sound of tires crunching on the stone and clay road interrupted her thoughts. Looking down at the road, she half expected to see the silver Intrepid returning to the house. But instead she saw a tan Jeep Cherokee drive slowly past her. On the side of the jeep in green lettering was a pine tree with the words PARK RANGER written in an arc above it. The man inside the jeep looked from one side of the road to the other, as if searching for something.

A few minutes after the jeep, Sara again heard a vehicle approaching. This time she was sure it would be Danny returning home from the store. And again, she was wrong. This time it was an old blue sedan that drove past her, at a slightly faster speed. Sara scarcely made out the figure of George Stine, looking even more distraught than he had the day before.

"I wonder what's going on?" Sara asked. It wasn't all that rare to see the Park Ranger take a drive from time to time to make sure everything was okay with the town. But the way he was looking at the road made Sara believe he had a more meaningful purpose than just going for a cruise. And then to see George Stine doing the same thing, it just seemed weird. Was it a coincidence? Sara didn't know but she suddenly began to hope that the next crunching sound she'd hear coming up the road would be her husband.

Chapter Twenty

The first thing Danny saw as he pulled up the drive was his wife standing out on the deck. Upon seeing the car, she waved down at him. After he parked, Danny grabbed the bags of groceries and headed up the stairway. Sara met him at the porch and held the door open for him. "How'd you make out?" she asked.

"Okay for the most part," he replied. "I bumped into Anna and she informed me that she and her date are meeting us at the B.Y.I. at seven."

"We didn't say for sure—"

"Save it," Danny said. "I already tried to tell her that. Besides, if we don't go I have a nagging suspicion they would end up knocking on our door anyway."

Sara smiled. "You're probably right. Oh well, it won't be that bad. It's only one night, we have the rest of the week still."

"I know," Danny said. "Anyway, we have a couple of hours to kill in the meantime. What would you like to do?"

"I thought about taking a trip to the museum," Sara answered. "You'd like it."

"Sounds fine to me," he said. "Let's put these groceries away and head on out."

*　　*　　*

The young couple turned onto the main road as if they were leaving town. Two miles down, Sara said, "Make this left coming up."

"Okay," Danny obliged. This new road continued for some time, surrounded by thick green forest on either side. Soon a brown building came into view.

"That's the ranger's station," Sara said.

"It is? Do you think we should stop by and mention that deer we found yesterday?" Danny asked.

"I was going to suggest that," Sara said. "But the park ranger isn't there right now. I just saw him drive by our house a couple of minutes ago."

"Oh, maybe we'll stop on the way home if there's time," he said.

"Yeah. Okay, you need to turn here," Sara said. Danny turned and a mile down on the right was the Promised Land Museum. "That's it over there." Danny parked the car next to an extremely small building.

"Are you sure this is it?" Danny asked. "It's kind of small."

"It just appears that way," Sara replied. "It's a lot bigger on the inside."

"Okay," Danny said as they made their way up the walk to the entrance. Sara swung open the small door and they entered into a room with a big fireplace directly in front of them. Next to the fireplace was an elderly lady sitting behind a tiny desk.

"Good afternoon," the lady smiled. "Come on in. My name is Edna, how are you today?"

"Fine, thank you," Sara said. "I'm Sara and this is Danny."

"Ain't that nice," Edna said. "Well, you'll have the whole place to yourselves. I haven't had one visitor yet today."

"Really?" Danny said.

"Yes sir," Edna replied. "This place will be packed pretty good come this weekend, but for the time being this is it. Well, go on and enjoy yourselves."

"Thank you," Sara said as they headed down a narrow hallway. This led into a slightly larger room. Around the perimeter of the room were exhibits of all kinds enclosed in glass cases. But it was the center of the room that attracted Danny's attention. Standing on a platform surrounded by a velvet rope was an extremely large bear. He walked over and looked at the animal with awe.

"That's a big bear," he said.

"Believe it or not," Sara said, "But they actually get bigger."

"You're kidding?"

"Nope."

"I'll take your word for it," Danny said, reading the information that was attached to a small podium nearby. "It says here her name was Elsie. She lived to be fourteen years old and weighed 429 pounds. Sounds like my old algebra teacher."

Sara laughed. "You're bad."

Moving toward the far wall, Danny noticed three large, black and white photographs, each with a small caption beneath them. Above the pictures in bold black letters it read: THE HISTORY OF PROMISED LAND. He walked over and looked at the first photo. It showed several men standing in an open field, some holding shovels while several others held pick axes. Danny read the caption beneath it.

The land that is now called Promised Land was once used as hunting grounds for the Minsi Tribe of the Wolf Clan of the Lenni-Lenape Indians. The local traditions say the land was promised to the religious group "the Shakers." The Shakers found the land far too rocky to be used as farmland and departed, sarcastically naming the grounds "The Promised Land."

"Hmm," Danny said, moving onto the next photo. This one showed a row of sawmills amongst a few patches of trees. He paused to continue reading.

The early settlers of the area built sawmills to process the large stands of conifer and hardwood trees. The land was repeatedly clear-cut. With all the activity came erosion, forest fires, and the migration of wildlife from the area.

Danny walked over to the third and final picture. He saw in this photograph a beautiful park, surrounded by a lush forest. He read the last caption.

In 1902, the Commonwealth of Pennsylvania purchased the land. They worked diligently to protect and reclaim the area and soon the forest and wildlife began to return. Promised Land became the fourth Pennsylvania state park.

Then in 1905, the first park facilities opened. Many additional facilities were built in the 1930's by the Civilian Conservation Corps (CCC) who also built roads, bridges and dams, and planted thousands of trees.

"Hey, honey," Danny called. "Where'd you go?"

"Over here," came the reply from another room nearby. "Check this out."

Danny followed his wife's voice down another hallway and into the largest room yet. Displays were everywhere, some even hanging down from the ceiling. "You were right, it *is* a lot bigger on the inside." He spotted Sara standing besides a large glass case. "Whatcha got here?"

"Ancient weapons," she replied. "Check out those primitive knives." Inside were crude metal pointed objects, attached to a wooden handle by some twine. "These were some of the weapons used by—"

"The Lenni-Lenape Indians," Danny interrupted.

Sara smiled. "Wow, I'm impressed."

"You better believe it, baby," he smirked.

"Okay, Einstein, let's look at a couple of more things but then we have to go," Sara said. "It's almost six o'clock."

"Oh, that's right," Danny said. "Our big double date."

"Be nice," Sara said. "It will be over before you know it."

"Says you," he replied. Danny wasn't sure why, but he had the feeling that they were going to be in for a very long night.

Chapter Twenty-One

The sun slowly started to set over the top of the Pocono Mountains. Small animals scurried to their nests while owls sat on their nightly perch.

Inside the cave, all was quiet. The darkness was thick, almost tangible. Nothing could be seen. Yet something was there. It moved slowly, through the second cavern and into the first. At the entrance it paused and sniffed the air heavily, its keen nostrils searching the area. Then with an ungodly roar, it melted into the night.

*   *   *

The smell of grilled chicken always made Harry Kinder's mouth water. It was a nice night and Susan had suggested a barbecue, to which he had wholeheartedly agreed, for Harry felt that the best meals he had ever tasted had come from the grill. He liked to watch the flames as they danced across the rack. Standing there in his backyard, almost mesmerized by the grill, he barely noticed the slight tugging on his sleeve.

"Daddy?"

Looking down, he saw his daughter's smiling face. "Yes, Stacy?"

"I'm hungry, is it almost ready?" she asked eagerly.

"Almost, honey," Harry smiled. "Just a few more minutes."

"Oh, daddy," Stacy whined.

"In the meantime, why don't you go and pick up all the toys you girls left throughout the yard today."

"Lisa left most of them!" Stacy exclaimed.

"Lisa is helping mommy set the table," he smiled at his five-year-old daughter. "Go on, by the time you finish up your dinner will be ready."

"Okay," she mumbled and walked away.

The Kinders' backyard was fairly large. It contained a swing set, slide and a playhouse. A chain-link fence surrounded the yard. Past the fence were thick trees and shrubbery, which continued for more than fifty yards until the next property.

Stacy grabbed a small red wagon, which she usually used to pull her sister around the yard with and, sighing loudly as possible, started the tedious task of collecting her toys. After a few minutes she had almost completely filled the wagon. Nodding her own approval she quickly scanned the yard to see if she had missed anything. Leaning against the fence on the far side of the yard was a small, pink sports car, which was used to transport her dolls. She could barely see the car because the patio light didn't reach that far back in the yard. Pulling her wagon behind her, Stacy walked the length of the yard and knelt down beside her toy. Laying the car flat, she took her Barbie doll from the wagon and placed her in the driver's seat. Next, she picked a male doll and placed him in the passenger's seat. "That's better," she declared.

As she said this, the shrubbery on the other side of the fence started to shake violently. Stacy looked up and tilted her head. Then she looked back at her father, who was two-dozen yards away. He looked up from the grill and waved at her.

Waving back, she directed her attention back toward the shrubs. The noises ceased. Then some branches on a nearby maple tree started to snap. With a quizzical look on her face, young Stacy Kinder approached the fence.

Chapter Twenty-Two

"Are you ready yet?" Danny's voice floated from the other side of the bathroom door. "I'm starving!"

"Okay," Sara replied and opened the door.

Danny was right on the other side, leaning against the wall. When she appeared, he straightened up. "Wow, you look nice." She was wearing a blue sundress, which matched her eye color perfectly.

"Thank you," Sara beamed. "You ready?"

"Let's go," he said as they headed toward the front door. "I hope the food is as good as you say it is. It might make up for the company."

"It won't be that bad," she replied. "Anna's okay in her own sort of hyper way. Besides, she'll be all wrapped up in this new stud of hers to bother you."

"Let's hope so," Danny said. They carefully made their way down the stairway and reached the car. He unlocked the passenger door and held it open for his wife.

"You're such a gentleman," she said as she slid inside.

"I know," he agreed.

He walked around to the driver's side of the car and was about to open the door when there came a loud thrashing sound from up toward the house. Danny paused with his hand on the handle, looking back up the steep stairway. The outside light attached to the shed shined brightly. Other than a few moths bouncing off the light, nothing stirred. Then there was a tapping noise. Danny looked down to see Sara's hand tapping the window. He opened the door. "What's wrong?" She asked.

"I heard something thrashing around up there," he answered.

"Oh, don't worry about it. It was probably a skunk or something."

"It sounded bigger than that."

"You wouldn't think so, but believe me sometimes the littlest animal can sound like an elephant when it runs through the shrubbery around here."

Danny took one last look up the slope and nodded. "You got my vote," he said and got into the car.

*   *   *

As he slid the Intrepid into a front parking space at the Barn Yard Inn, Danny looked around the lot with surprise. "Cars," he said sarcastically.

"Of course," Sara replied. "It's dinner time, half the town comes here this time of night."

"Oh."

As they entered the inn Danny grabbed Sara's hand proudly. Directly in front of them was the bar, where a balding man was waiting on an elderly gentleman. To the right was the dining area. Spread throughout the large room was wooden tables and chairs, all with napkins folded and silverware shining. The room was mildly crowded, everyone seeming to be having a good time. But it was the table closest to the entrance that they saw Anna. She was engrossed in a conversation with a muscular young man with dirty blonde hair when she glanced up and saw them.

"Oh, hi!" Anna said, leaping to her feet.

"Hi, Anna," Sara replied and Danny nodded.

"Sara, I would like you to meet Brad Thompson," Anna said, beaming with pride. "Brad, this is my good friend Sara Evans."

"Walker," Danny corrected.

"What? Oh yeah, Walker," Anna said. "Sorry. Sara Walker. I'm still not used to you being married yet, girl."

"Nice to meet you," Sara said.

"Nice to meet you too," Brad said, extending his hand.

Shaking his hand Sara said, "And this is my husband Danny."

"Hi," Danny said as they too exchanged a handshake.

As they sat down, a slender woman approached them. "Hi, folks, would you like something to drink?"

Sara looked up to see Joanne Simpson. "Hi, Joanne."

"Well, Sara Evans, it's good to see you again!"

"Walker," Danny corrected again.

"Excuse me?" Joanne said.

"Um, my last name is now Walker," Sara said.

"What? Don't tell me little Sara Evans got married?"

"Yes, I did," she replied.

"Well, congratulations, sweetie," Joanne said as she leaned down and gave Sara a big hug. "That's wonderful. And you must be the lucky man," Joanne said, turning her attention to Danny.

"Guilty as charged," he replied. "I'm Danny Walker."

"Joanne Simpson," she said. "It's a pleasure to meet you."

"Likewise—" Danny started to say.

"Joanne, I would like you to meet Brad Thompson," Anna cut in, smiling.

"Oh, nice to meet you, Brad," Joanne said.

"Same here," Brad said, his face reddening slightly.

"Well, you make sure Anna stays out of trouble," Joanne said, with a slight hint of seriousness in her voice.

"Yes, ma'am," Brad replied.

"Isn't he a dream?" Anna said, making Brad's face go from light red to dark.

"Anyway," Joanne said, whipping out a pad of paper. "What will you have to drink?" As she said this, another customer entered the bar. Danny turned around to see the face of George Stine staring straight at him.

Chapter Twenty-Three

S tacy Kinder stopped in front of the fence. Being only five years old, she was much shorter than the chain-linked obstacle. Standing on her tiptoes, she squinted to see what was making all the noise, but it was too dark to see anything in the dense shrubbery. But she could *sense* something was there. She peered into the growing darkness the best she could. As she stood there, she was suddenly grabbed and lifted off the ground.

"Hi, pumpkin," Harry said, resting her in his arms. "What are you doing?"

Looking back toward the bushes, she responded, "Nothing. Is dinner ready yet?"

"It sure is," he smiled and carried her away.

*   *   *

Placing the chicken in the center, Harry Kinder took his seat at the head of the table. His wife Susan sat at the opposite end while the girls sat cross from each other. "Let's say grace."

"Grace!" the girls said in unison.

Susan smiled over at her husband, who was trying hard not to laugh. "Very funny. Lisa, will you say grace tonight?"

"Okay," she said. "Everybody close their eyes." As they did so,

Lisa cleared her throat loudly and began. "Dear Lord, thank you for mommy, daddy and Stacy. And thank you for our food, Amen."

"Amen," the rest of the family said.

As they began to pass around the dishes, Mr. Kinder stood up, grabbing a spatula.

"Where are you going, daddy?" Lisa asked.

"I have to go and check on the rest of the chicken," he replied. As he said this, there came a loud crash from outside. Susan stood up and looked at her husband with concern. "Stay here," he said and headed toward the back door.

Instinctively holding the spatula like some kind of weapon, Harry opened the back door and stepped outside into the brightly lit patio. Immediately he saw the grill, still smoking, lying on its side. The lid had been ripped off, with the rack laying a few yards away. He didn't see any signs of chicken remaining. Looking up, he surveyed the yard. His head slowly shifted from left to right as he scanned the dark yard. Then he stopped. At the back of the yard, exactly where Stacy had been standing, there was a section of the fence missing.

Frowning, he took several steps forward. "What the—" He now noticed that the fence wasn't missing at all—it was *smashed*. It looked as though a steamroller had made a path right through that portion of the chain-link fence. Then it suddenly dawned on him that he was standing in the middle of his yard holding a spatula. He quickly started to backtrack. As he started to turn around, something grabbed him. Harry yelped and spun around. It was Susan.

"Harry? Is everything okay?" Susan asked.

"Yeah, everything's okay," he replied, quickly recovering. "Something smelled the chicken is all, probably a small black bear or something."

"Are you sure?"

"Yeah, I'm sure."

"Okay," she said. Then, she saw the fence. "Harry—"

"Come on," he said, leading her back toward the house. "Let's get inside."

Chapter Twenty-Four

Looking at the four young people, George crossed his arms and sneered. After a moment, he turned and took a seat at the bar. "Hey, Tom," he said, gesturing to the bartender. "Gimme the usual." Then he turned back and winked at Danny.

"Friend of yours?" Brad asked.

"Not exactly," Danny replied.

"Old George Stine," Joanne said, shaking her head. "Don't let him bother you, Danny. His bark is worse than his bite."

"He doesn't," Danny said as he turned back around.

For the next hour they talked and ate their meal, which to Danny's delight was very good. Anna controlled most of the conversation, which went from her parents, to her money, to sex and back again. Poor Brad didn't say a word all night and seemed way too timid for Anna's taste. But she clung to his massive arm the whole time nonetheless. "Daddy always used to say to me," Anna was saying, "You can't sit like that with a skirt on!" She laughed loudly while everyone else seemed to think it was less than amusing.

"So, Brad," Danny cut in. "Where are you from?"

"Indiana," Anna answered for him.

"Really? What brings you up here?" Sara asked.

This time Brad was allowed to answer. "Well, right now I'm living with my father on the outskirts of Canadensis. My folks just got separated after twenty-seven years of marriage."

"I'm sorry to hear that," Danny said. Danny assumed it must be much more difficult to deal with your parents' separation at Brad's age than when his own parents split up.

"Yeah," Brad said. "It's been rough, but we're getting through it."

"Well, take it from me—" Danny started to say when there was a tap on his shoulder. Turning around, he saw George standing there, smiling. "What?"

"I just wanted to bid you kiddies a good night," he said. He had had more than a couple of drinks.

"Yeah well, good night," Danny retorted. "Try not to run anybody else off the road this time."

"What?" George stammered. "What'd you say?"

"You heard me," Danny said sternly.

"You looking for trouble?" George asked angrily.

At this point the massive body of Brad Thompson stood up. "Are you?" he asked, cracking his knuckles.

George stood there for a moment, taking in the size of the young man before him. "Um—"

"George Stine!" Joanne walked briskly over to the drunken man. "Will you leave these poor kids alone? I've told you before about making trouble in my place."

George stared at Brad and smiled. "I was only playing with them."

"Well, play time is over," Joanne replied. "Why don't you go hang out with Henry?"

"I can't," George said, lowering his voice. "He's missing."

"Say again," Joanne said, annoyed.

"I said he's missing."

"Maybe he's working late," said Joanne.

"No, he's not working late," George snapped. "He's been missing since yesterday. His car is still in the driveway but he's not home."

"Well, then he's curled up drunk somewhere—"

"No, he's not."

Joanne sighed. "Did you tell Allan?"

"Yeah, I stopped by earlier," George said calmly. "He searched for him all day, I made sure of it."

"Yeah, I saw you," Sara said.

George nodded. "Around five he headed up the mountain. He told me I couldn't tag along, on the count of all those dead deer."

"There was more than one?" Danny found himself asking. "I mean, we found one yesterday."

"Listen, George, I'm sure your buddy is just fine," Joanne said. "Why don't you try his house one more time? Maybe he was sleeping and didn't hear you?"

George opened his mouth to protest again but then he stopped. "Okay, I'll try one more time." Then he turned and left the bar.

"Sorry about that," Joanne said.

"No need to apologize," Anna said cheerfully. "We had my bodyguard here to protect us." With this statement, Brad's face once again turned bright red and he quickly sat down.

Joanne smiled. "Will there be anything else?"

Chapter Twenty-Five

As he drove slowly along the road, George kept a constant eye out for his lost companion. The whole town always thought of Henry as a drunk, but that wasn't necessarily true. He's just been through a lot of rough times. George knew of Henry's background and how he moved up here after his wife up and left him out of the clear blue. Nobody else knew Henry the way that George did; he was his best friend.

When he reached Henry's trailer, he pulled over and walked up the dirt path to the front door. "Henry?" George called, banging on the door. Looking to his left, he saw that Henry's car was still in the driveway. "Yo, Henry, you in there?" Silence was all that answered him. "Henry?" Getting no response again, he turned and peered in the window, but it was too dark to clearly see anything.

Disappointed, George returned to his car. As he drove, he noticed a light fog start to cover the road. As the fog thickened, his mind started forming shapes in the swirling mist. Then sounds accompanied the shapes. Then suddenly he was back in that horrible room. Then the sound began. The sound he would remember for the rest of his life. That excruciating beep that announced his wife Edith had taken her last breath. *Flatline*. That is what the nurse kept saying as she shoved him out of the way. Then doctors were swarming everywhere, pumping her heart repeatedly, but to no avail. Cancer. Colon cancer that had spread rapidly to her bones. *Unusually fast*, the doctors all agreed, *especially for a woman of only forty-five years*. As George's eyes swelled up with tears, the images vanished and before him once again was just thick fog.

He continued until he reached a stop sign. He could go only left or right. If he turned left, it would take him back toward the main road. If he turned right, it would take him toward his own home. George sat and thought for a moment. Maybe he should go around once more, to see if his friend was stumbling home from somewhere. But he thought it was probably a lost cause. If Henry were passed out somewhere George would never be able to find him. George finally decided that out of the two of them, Henry was the one sleeping soundly somewhere while he was out driving around. So, he turned right.

As he did so, the car's headlights shined brightly into the darkness. They illuminated a house, a mailbox, a small bush and—*something*.

"What was that?" George exclaimed, skidding to a stop. Leaping out of his car, he saw a large dark form dart quickly behind the house. George took several steps forward, the red clay and stone crunching beneath his feet. He stood there silently, his headlights cutting the night in two.

"I know I'm a little drunk," George whispered to himself. "But I know I saw something and that sure wasn't no black bear." He stood there in the middle of the street, staring at the dark house. He stayed that way for several minutes. He finally turned to leave and then stopped short. He still didn't see anything, but he *heard* something. It was a familiar crunching sound. George looked down at his feet— they weren't moving. Something else was walking on the road.

George was standing only a few feet from his blue sedan. He turned to his right and looked out into the darkness, but didn't see anything. He quickly turned to his left—nothing. But the crunching sounds were getting louder. Not only louder, George realized, but faster too. George turned in a complete circle—the noises seemed to come from every direction. Instinctively, he turned and sprinted to his car. George caught movement out of the corner of his eye but kept on going. Reaching the car, he flung open the door and dove in. He slammed the door shut and locked it.

As he started to turn the key, something rammed the car. The impact was tremendous, spinning the car almost completely around. George, who was now crying, tried turning the ignition. The sedan sputtered but didn't start. "Come on!" he cried, pumping the gas pedal. He tried again and was met with the same result. "Please! Come on!"

As he tried a fourth time, he became aware of more crunching sounds coming rapidly toward him. "No!" George cried, turning the ignition one last time. This time the car roared to life and just before another impact, he slammed the gear into drive and sped away.

Chapter Twenty-Six

Anna spooned the last of her vanilla ice cream into her mouth and sighed. "Wow, that really hit the spot." Danny stared at her in amazement. He thought that *he* was a heavy eater, but Anna Morris continued to eat twenty minutes after Danny could no longer consume any more. If you were to look at her slender figure, you'd think she hardly ate at all. "So, Danny, how'd you like the food here?"

"It was very good," he replied. "You obviously enjoyed yours?"

"Absolutely," Anna replied, failing to note the sarcasm. "Hasn't this been fun?"

"It sure has," Sara answered before Danny had an opportunity to. "We'll have to do it again sometime."

"Sure," Danny said. "On our twenty-fifth wedding anniversary—"

"Sure," Anna said, smiling broadly. "Before you guys leave we'll get together again."

"It's been real nice meeting you folks," Brad said.

"Brad, the pleasure was ours," Danny said. He meant that comment. From the little time they spent with him, Brad Thompson seemed like an all around nice guy, way too nice for Anna's standards anyhow.

"Say," Anna exclaimed, "Why don't you guys come back to my place for a while? We can have a few drinks and go swimming in my pool—"

"As tempting as that sounds," Danny interrupted, "We're probably going to call it a night."

"Really?" Anna asked, looking at Sara like a lost puppy dog. "Are you sure?"

"Yeah," Sara agreed. "It's after nine already and it's been a long day—"

"I know," Anna winked. "You're newlyweds and you need to go do newlywed stuff."

"On that note," Brad said as the two couples stood up. "Have a good night."

As they said their good-byes, the door to the inn flew open and in stumbled George Stine.

Chapter Twenty-Seven

Allan Parker's flashlight swayed from side to side. Even though the month of September was right around the corner, it was still very hot. He paused momentarily to wipe the sweat from his brow. He had searched in town until four-thirty and then after a quick dinner, headed up the mountain.

Henry was known to occupy some of the trails along the bottom half of the mountain from time to time, scaring hikers half to death. Allan knew that Bill Darley had done the same route yesterday morning, but Allan hoped to see something that Bill might have missed.

Unfortunately, he did not. Not only was Allan hoping to find Henry, he was also hoping to find some evidence as to what was killing all the wildlife in Promised Land. But because of the lack of rain they've had, Allan wasn't able to find a single track and because of the tornado, broken trees' limbs were a common sight.

He started up the mountain when there was still plenty of daylight. But he quickly had lost track of time and now as he made his way back down, the only light he had was from the flashlight he had decided to bring along with him.

He continued down the trail, looking for any signs that might help him in solving the mystery. He had reached a fork in the path when something suddenly reflected off his flashlight.

Allan paused and shined his light to his right. He saw it again a few yards off the trail. Keeping his light on the object, he walked over and picked it up. In his hand was a silver Coors Light beer can.

Allan studied the forest around him. Then he saw it. Partially hidden behind a clump of hemlock trees sat a yellow tent. As he drew closer to the tent more beer cans came into view. "Hello there," Allan called. "Henry?" Only an owl answered him. Then he spotted a pair of backpacks. "I'm sorry to inform you but these trails are temporarily closed." As he got closer he noticed a small campfire was all set to go, but was never lighted. "Hello?"

He wasn't able to see the condition of the tent until he was right up on it. Huge rips covered it, as if someone had taken a chainsaw to it. The front flaps of the tent were open. Using his flashlight to push aside the right flap, he peered inside. "Hello?"

He only looked for a moment. Then he quickly turned, fell to his knees, and vomited.

Chapter Twenty-Eight

"What now?" Danny muttered as George looked wildly around the room. "What's wrong with him?"

Sara eyed George carefully. "It looks as though he's seen a ghost."

"Well, we're not waiting around to find out," Anna said, grabbing Brad by the arm. "We'll see you guys later."

"See you later," Brad said as he was dragged toward the door.

As they made their way past George, he suddenly grabbed Anna's arm. "No! Don't go out there!" he gasped.

"Let go of me you creep!" Anna yelled, getting the attention of Joanne Simpson.

"George!" Joanne exclaimed, walking sternly over to him. "I thought I told you to leave. Didn't you find Henry?"

George shook his head. He opened his mouth but no sound came out. "Is he okay?" Danny asked.

Sara looked at Danny and then back at George. "Maybe he should sit down."

Joanne led him to the nearest barstool. "Tom," she said to the bartender who had just come through the swinging doors that led to the kitchen. "Bring me a glass of water." Tom quickly obliged.

George grabbed the glass and gulped down its contents. He held the glass out and Joanne placed it on the bar. "Now, what's wrong?"

"There's a monster outside," he croaked.

Danny and Sara exchanged glances, while Anna let out an irritable sigh. Joanne looked at Tom, who was trying hard not to burst out into laughter. "A monster?"

"I had just passed Henry's place when this thing ran out in front of me—"

"What did it look like?" Joanne asked, as if she were asking a child.

"I don't know, I only caught a glimpse," George replied, speaking a little more clearly. "But it was definitely *big*."

"I'm sure you did," Joanne said soothingly. "Look, George, you had a few drinks, right? And the night can play tricks on you—"

"You don't believe me?" George exclaimed, jumping up. "It rammed my car—go see for yourself!"

"Great idea," Anna groaned as she grabbed Brad by the arm and headed out the door. "See ya, Sara."

"I'm sure it did," Joanne said.

"Don't patronize me," George snapped, regaining his composure. "I'm telling you and I'm telling everyone in here that there's something out there. If you don't want to listen to me that's fine." Then he turned and stared right at Danny and Sara. "It's your funeral."

Chapter Twenty-Nine

A llan sat motionless, his mind going a mile a minute. For a split second he thought he was back at his office, asleep in that swivel chair of his. Any minute now he'd wake up and discover that this was all just a horrible nightmare. He looked up at the sky and took several deep breaths. As a former cop he'd seen plenty of grisly deaths before. But nothing like this. After regaining his composure, he reluctantly turned back around.

From what he could tell, there were two corpses. It was difficult to say for they were badly mangled. One was hanging halfway out a huge tear in the back of the tent, as if there was a last ditch effort to escape.

The other was closer to the center of the tent and had been ripped in half just below the waist, the intestines clearly visible. He shined the light onto the victim's face. "Oh no—" Even though it was dark and the face was distorted and bloody, there was no mistaking who the unfortunate individual was. Allan was staring into the face of his own deputy, Bill Darley.

Chapter Thirty

George continued to stare at the young couple. "Well," Danny said, grabbing Sara's hand. "We'd better get going."

As they started to pass him, George stepped in front of the newlyweds. "Listen, kid, take the little lady here and get out of town."

"George!" Joanne snapped. "Let them mercifully go home!"

George slowly stepped aside, but Danny lingered a moment longer, studying the middle-aged man. George's face showed no signs of this being a joke. His eyes seemed to beg Danny to believe him. Then, they turned and left.

"Okay, George," Joanne said. "Your turn, time to go home."

"No please," George begged. "Let me stay. It's almost closing time, just let me stay until then."

Joanne eyed George over and sighed. "Okay, George, you can stay. Just no more talk of monsters, deal?"

George started to protest, but then quickly closed his mouth. "Deal," he muttered and took a seat at the bar. "I need a drink."

Outside, Sara started walking toward the Intrepid but Danny was walking the opposite way. "Danny?"

"Hold on," he said, talking over his shoulder. "I want to check this out." He stopped in front of the old blue sedan, kneeled down, and whistled. "Wow."

"What is it?" Sara asked, walking up behind him. "Oh, that's what." The whole side of the car was so badly buckled, it looked as though a wrecking ball had hit it. Directly in the center of the damage, was a small blot of blood.

"Well," Danny said, standing up. "I don't know about monsters, but something sure did a number on it."

*   *   *

As they drove down the dark streets toward their house, Sara racked her brain as to what George could have hit with his car. "Maybe he hit a telephone pole."

"I've never seen one that bled before," Danny replied.

"If he hit an animal, he would have had to hit it head on, not from the side," Sara said. "And the dent was huge—it had to have been a bear."

"And it just got up and walked away afterward?" Danny said, slightly smiling. "That doesn't make sense."

"Okay, then you give me a better explanation," she said.

"No problem," Danny replied. Then after a moment, he said, "It was a monster."

As they made the left turn that led to their house, another pair of headlights blinded them. Danny slowed as the other vehicle flicked off their high beams and stopped beside them. Danny rolled down the driver's side window as the other vehicle rolled down theirs. Then, the strangers flicked on their interior light.

"Mr. Kinder?" Danny asked.

"Hi, Danny, hi, Sara," he replied.

"Where are you guys going this late at night?" Sara asked.

Harry Kinder glanced at his daughters in the back seat. They were playing quietly. "We're taking the kids to see their grandmother in Allentown."

Then, Mr. Kinder unbuckled his seat belt and stepped out of his van. Leaning into the Intrepid's window, he spoke softly. "I didn't want to alarm the kids."

"Alarm them about what?" Sara asked.

"This evening during dinner, *something* attacked our grill," he said.

"Your grill?" Danny asked.

"Yes. We were having chicken and while we were inside, something went through our fence and tore apart our grill."

"You mean went over your fence?" Sara asked.

"No, I mean went *through* our fence," Harry replied sternly. "It had to have been a bear. I mean, what else could it have been? But judging by the hole in the fence, it would have to have been a bear of considerable size. Black bears can get big, but not that big. This may seem silly, but we feel it might be safer to take the kids away for a while, just until school starts up again. It will do them some good to get out of town for a while anyway. Susan's mother gets lonely sometimes and she was very excited to hear that we were coming for a visit." He paused for a moment. "I know this all sounds weird, but if something is running around out here—just be careful, okay?"

"It doesn't sound all that weird," Danny said. "No more weird than what George Stine just told us."

"George Stine?" Harry said, a quizzical look on his face.

"He just finished telling us that a monster attacked him in his car," Sara said. "He was pretty shaken."

"Yeah," Danny said. "His car looks like your fence; all banged up."

Harry lowered his head and seemed to be deep in thought. Then, he said, "I know this is your honeymoon, but it might be wise to spend it somewhere else."

"Harry?" Susan called. "Is everything okay?"

"Yes, dear," he replied. Then to the couple he said, "We've got to get going. Take care of yourselves."

"We will," Sara said. "Thank you."

"Yeah, thanks," Danny said as Harry Kinder got back into his van. Then, the interior light blinked out and the Kinders continued down the road.

Chapter Thirty-One

The silence of the night was broken by the soft beat of music. The backyard was literally bright as day, thanks to the outdoor lights spread throughout the massive property. In the center of the yard was the swimming pool, the lights making the water glimmer. It was rectangular shaped, with a diving board at the far end.

The house was huge, boasting three stories. Windows made up most of the outside exterior; it was quite impressive. Brad Thompson smiled. "This is some place you got here."

"It's all right," Anna replied nonchalantly. Everybody said that their first time there. "It can get lonely though."

"Oh."

"I mean, usually I have parties here all the time," she said. "But this week everybody was busy. I wasn't even planning on coming up this week but my mother wanted me out of her hair for another one of her boring social gatherings."

"Really?" Brad said, not knowing exactly what to say.

"Yep," Anna said, apparently not noticing his apprehension. "And my father, he always takes me on these big yachts for these stupid fishing trips with all of these big wig types—it's awful."

"Sounds awful," Brad lied. To him, that didn't sound awful at all. His idea of a fun filled night was sitting on the porch, drinking some beers with his father.

"It really is," Anna continued, without missing a beat. "He's always saying, 'Now, sweetheart, remember to act like a lady today.' Ugh!"

"Aren't you?"

"Aren't I what?"

"A lady."

Anna smiled. "When I want to be."

She was about to say something else when something behind her got Brad's attention. "Oh wow," he said, walking past her. A dozen yards behind the pool was an extremely large oak tree. "Look at the size of this."

"Oh that," Anna said, clearly disappointed. "That stupid old thing. My mother wants to cut it down but my father refuses. He says that it's real old or something."

"You bet it is," Brad said, looking up. "That's at least fifty feet tall. When I was a kid, I used to love to climb these bad boys." Having said that, he reached out and grabbed the lowest limb of the tree. Then, he pulled himself up until he was sitting on it. "This is great. Care to join me?"

"No, thanks," Anna scoffed. "It probably has ticks or something."

Brad laughed. "Ticks?"

"Yes, ticks," Anna said, slightly annoyed. "Didn't you have them back in Indiana?" Then, she cooled down. "Besides, I can think of something better you can do with your hands."

Brad swung down and walked over to her. "Like what?"

"Oh, I don't know," she smiled, sliding her hands up and down Brad's muscular arms. "We'll think of something."

As she closed in on him to kiss him, there came a tremendous commotion in the woods to their left. Anna's yard did not have a fence. There were small bushes planted as a natural perimeter throughout the yard and then the forest took over. "What was that?" Brad asked.

"Who cares?" Anna said. "Maybe it was Yogi Bear."

They were about to kiss again when suddenly out of the forest ran several whitetail deer. They ran right past the stunned couple and kept on going, not slowing for a moment. Then they disappeared into the shrubbery on the opposite side of the yard. "Okay," Anna said. "That was interesting."

"What got into them?" Brad asked, walking over to the edge of the property. He peered into the deep foliage, but it was too dark to see. "I can't see anything. Say, what do you think George was rambling on about back at the bar?"

Anna, losing her patience, said, "I don't care about that drunk George Stine or what's gotten into the deer, I'm more concerned about what I can get into *me*."

That got Brad's attention. He swiftly walked back over to her and, leaning down, kissed her heavily. After a few moments, they parted and Anna asked, "Have you ever made love in a pool before?"

Brad shook his head. "No."

"Good," Anna said. "Believe me, it's quite exhilarating."

Brad looked down at the pool and then back at Anna. As he stood there, Brad started to wonder how many other guys Anna had asked this very same question to. But considering the feeling he had swelling up inside him, he pushed the thought out of his mind and said, "Then let's do it."

"You got it," Anna said, smiling broader than she had all night long.

Chapter Thirty-Two

Allan shined his flashlight onto the backpacks that stood beside the tent. Unzipping one, he fished in and pulled out several objects: a pack of cards, a comb—and a wallet. Opening it up, he found the driver's license. "Hmm," Allan murmured. "Charles Madison." Allan thought for a moment and then remembered Bill always talking about his friend Charlie. Allan had never met Charlie before . . . until now.

Then Allan took one last look inside the tent. As he was about to turn around, he noticed something in the corner that he had missed before. He reached in and picked up the object. It was Bill's trusty Remington 12-gauge shotgun, Old Betsy. Allan cracked it open and peered into the chamber. It was fully loaded. Bill never had a chance to grab his weapon. Allan snapped the gun shut. "Bill," he said out loud. "Why? Why did you have to try and play the hero?"

Just then, the bushes to his left started to sway back and forth and some branches started to snap. Allan still had his .45 tucked under his belt but since he was already holding the larger weapon, he kept it. He crouched down and clicked off the safety. Crunching sounds could now be clearly heard—something was coming.

Chapter Thirty-Three

Tom Reimer handed George another glass of rum and coke. "Thanks," George mumbled.

"No problem," Tom replied. He actually found himself feeling sorry for George Stine. Once you got to him, he wasn't all *that* bad. Sure he and Henry Watson were considered the town's drunks, but they never really caused any serious trouble before and they usually stuck to themselves.

All Tom really knew about George was that his wife, Edith, had died young and that he never did recover from it. He had pretty much given up on life, since in George's mind life had given up on him.

"Tom," George said quietly. "You believe me, don't you?"

Tom had waited on George hundreds of times and he knew that George wasn't the type of person to make up stories. But at the same time, George did have a lot to drink tonight and it does get very dark on those roads sometimes. He tried to come up with a decent answer, but all that came out was, "I believe that you believe you saw something."

"I guess you don't," George grunted.

"George—"

"That's okay, Tom," George cut in. "I don't blame you for not believing me. After all, I'm only George Stine, the drunk, right?"

"Awe, come on, George," Tom said. "You know I don't feel that way."

"Well, you should," George continued. "It's true, isn't it? I'm just hallucinating and Henry is really off drunk somewhere . . ." After he mentioned Henry, George suddenly looked saddened. He raised his rum and coke and said, "To Henry."

Tom didn't know what to do. So, he grabbed a glass and filled it halfway with beer. "To Henry."

For the first time in history, George and Tom downed their drinks together. When they finished, George looked at Tom and said, "I'll tell you one thing. I hope I *am* wrong. I hope to God that I'm wrong."

Chapter Thirty-Four

T he sound of debris being crushed grew louder. Allan was positioned on one knee, his left hand clamped on the gun and light, while the right was on the trigger.

Suddenly a pair of eyes reflected off the light. *This is it,* he thought. His heart was in his throat. Sweat poured down his face. Then, out of the bushes, something emerged.

Allan aimed his weapon, ready to fire. Then he slowly lowered the gun and gave a big sigh of relief. Standing before him was a small black bear. As it took several steps forward, Allan noticed that it was only a cub. Surprisingly, it walked right up to him.

Allan knew that the best way to get killed was to mess with a black bear's cub, but for some unknown reason Allan didn't think that in this particular case that would be a problem. "Hey, little fellow," he said. "You're out late. Where are you going? Where's your mommy?"

The bear looked at him sadly, as if he understood the question. Then the cub slowly turned and walked off into the darkness. Allan hoped that the cub's mother was still around somewhere, but had a bad feeling that she wasn't. "You be careful out there."

Allan held the gun tightly and looked one last time at his former deputy. He had to get back to town. This was too big for him now. He needed to call the state police and inform them that there have been at least two murders, maybe more. But first he needed to warn everybody. He needed to tell the people that there was something new in town. Allan Parker had to tell them that the devil had come to Promised Land.

Chapter Thirty-Five

The blue Ford Escape whizzed along Interstate 80 at nearly ninety miles per hour. The driver's stomach was upset, had been ever since he left that sleazy diner just outside of Allentown. He made up his mind right then and there never to eat their meatloaf ever again.

He glanced down at the binders and notebooks lying on the passenger's side seat and his stomach churned twice as much. He dared not give thought to what was in the back of the SUV, for thinking of those objects would surely make him lose his dinner.

Ahead of him, a bright green sign reflected off his headlights: PROMISED LAND-45 MILES. After seeing this, the man spoke out loud. "I hope it isn't true. But if by some chance it is, God help them . . ."

*   *   *

Joanne Simpson walked up to the barstool where George Stine somberly sat. "Well," she said, "That's the last of the restaurant crowd. The bar will be closing down soon, too."

"I know," George mumbled.

"Listen, George, why don't you head on home—"

"You promised," George said, straightening up. "Until closing time."

"You're right," Joanne said. "Okay."

Just then Tom Reimer came through the swinging double doors from the kitchen. Noticing Joanne talking to George, he said, "Joanne, can I see you for a minute?"

"Sure," Joanne answered as she walked over to the opposite end of the bar. "What's up?"

"I think I should cut George off. I know he's been through a, um, dramatic experience tonight," Tom said, trying to find the right words. "But he's had enough."

"Good idea," she replied, stealing a quick glance back at George. "He's definitely toasted."

"You know," Tom said, "You handled him very well tonight."

"Oh," Joanne smirked. "Thanks. I know how to handle him."

"Not just him," Tom continued, looking down at the bar. "You handle every situation you're in so cool, calm and collective."

"Oh, I don't know about that," Joanne smiled.

"I admire that quality in you," he said.

"Thanks, Tom," Joanne said, suddenly noticing how nervous he was. "That means a lot."

"Really?" Tom said as he began to slightly fidget. "Well, I mean it."

"Well, I appreciate it. You know, being a woman on my own in an overall male environment like this can be tough sometimes."

"I'm sure it can be," Tom agreed.

"But It's nice to know that I'm appreciated."

"You are."

"Tom?" Joanne said.

"Yes?"

"You want to know something?"

"Sure," he replied.

"You're cute when you blush."

Chapter Thirty-Six

W*hat? What could have possibly done that? What?* Allan's mind was racing almost as fast as his feet. He plunged down the pitch-black trail, the small flashlight leading the way. *It couldn't have been a bear,* he thought. *No American black bear was capable of that. No, this was something else. But what?* As hard as he tried, he couldn't come up with an answer.

Well, I'll worry about that later, he thought. *Right now I need to warn whomever I can and call the state police. I need to tell them that something is running around tearing people to shreds.*

Just then, Allan had a hopeful thought. *Maybe it won't even head toward town. Just maybe, it won't.*

*   *   *

Stripped down to just his boxers, Brad Thompson dove head first into the pool. He quickly swam underwater from the deep end to the shallow. Then he surfaced, shaking his head from left to right. "Your turn," he smiled.

"Wow," Anna said, looking at the way the surrounding lights reflected off Brad's wet, muscular chest. "You're such a hunk."

"Thanks," he grinned, still feeling slightly embarrassed.

"Oh, you're quite welcome," Anna said, slipping out of her shoes.

"I've been waiting for this all night."

"Then don't delay," he replied.

"Tell you what," Anna said with a devious smile. "Swim back down to the deep end but this time go all the way to the bottom."

"Huh?"

"Trust me. Then I'll dive down in all my nakedness and meet you and we'll kiss all the way to the surface."

"Um, okay. If that's what you really want," Brad said hesitantly.

"Trust me, Brad," she giggled. "It's a really cool rush."

"Okay," Brad replied as he once again began to wonder how many other guys had done this very same thing. "Well, here goes nothing," he said and went under.

*   *   *

Allan Parker paused to catch his breath as he reached the area on the trail where the forest met the flatland caused by the tornado. He quickly glanced back toward the dark trees, wondering if something was watching him at that very moment.

Shaking loose those thoughts, he turned back around. Ahead in the distance, a little over a mile, was the main road where his Jeep was parked. Lights just to the right him caught his eye. It was the Barn Yard Inn. "I'll quickly stop in there first," he decided and started to run.

*   *   *

Upon reaching the bottom, Brad anxiously squinted upward, anticipating the naked flesh that would soon be swimming down to meet him.

Several seconds went by. And then, several more. He was just beginning to wonder how much longer he could hold his breath when the long awaited splash came.

That was a small splash, Brad thought. *Even for Anna*. It only took him one second to figure out why. It wasn't Anna that was sinking down to greet him . . . *it was her arm*. The water was just starting to turn bright red when Brad let out a gurgled scream and shot to the surface.

After taking a huge gulp of air, Brad quickly wiped his eyes and looked up to see Anna, covered in blood and suspended in mid-air by . . . *something*. Brad couldn't tell what it was because Anna's body blocked a good portion of it, but it was on its hind legs and it was *huge*. "Anna!"

Anna seemed to recognize her name and for a brief second her eyes met his. "B-Brad . . ." In the next instant the creature swiped it's massive claw and Anna Morris was torn completely in half, her torso landing in the water directly in front of Brad.

"Anna!"

Then the creature dropped down to all fours and casually walked over to the side of the pool. Brad couldn't believe what he was looking at. It was something straight out of a horror movie. *Was it a bear?* It resembled one, but it had fur in some places while others were wet and scaly. One eye was red, the other was yellow, and those teeth . . . He stayed as low to the water as he could, while trying to tread as quiet as possible.

Even though he was too terrified to even blink, he couldn't help but glimpse down at the torso of his would-be lover, floating up and down on the water like some giant bobber.

The creature just stood there, staring right at him, as if it was studying him. Then, with a tremendous growl, it lunged into the water.

Brad let out a high-pitched scream and frantically swam to the other side of the pool, away from the house. As he began to hoist himself out of the water, he could feel something directly under him. "Come on!" Brad cried as he raised his legs out of the pool.

As soon as he was out, he began to sprint. This side of the yard was wide open; there was nothing . . . except that huge oak tree. He hadn't gone more than four yards when there came a thunderous explosion from behind him, as the creature sprang out of the water. "Faster!" Brad urged himself as he ran toward the tree.

It's only six yards away. Five. Four. Brad was running so fast he barely noticed the pounding of the ground from the creature that was quickly gaining on him. *Three yards to go.* If he could make it to the tree, he could climb it all the way to the top, just like he used to do as a child. *Two.* He could almost feel the creature's breath on his back. *One yard to go . . . got it!* Brad grabbed the big, bottom branch of the tree and swung his legs swiftly up and to the left, snagging himself above the ground.

With the momentum far too great, the large creature ran right under him, stopping five yards past the oak tree.

Wasting no time, Brad was already climbing as fast as he possibly could, being careful in the process not to lose his footing. He was about thirty feet up when the tree below him started to shake violently. Pausing to glance down, Brad saw the unthinkable. Claw over claw, the creature was scurrying up the tree toward him. "No!" he screamed and started to climb again.

As fast as he climbed, it was still only a matter of seconds before the creature caught up to him. With a victorious roar it sunk its teeth deep into Brad's neck, dousing the old tree with blood. Then, with Brad Thompson locked firmly in its massive jaws, it leapt from the tree.

As the ground rushed to meet him, Brad had one final thought: *So this was the monster George was talking about . . .*

Chapter Thirty-Seven

E ver since they returned home from dinner, Sara Walker couldn't sit still. She paced from the dining room to the kitchen, then into the living room, where Danny sat in one of the recliners. "Sara, you've probably paced over a mile already," he said.

"I know," she sighed, slumping into the other recliner. "It's just that I've been coming up here my whole life and I've never even heard of anything like this happening before. Cars are being attacked, grills being destroyed, I mean, what's going on here?"

"I have no idea," Danny said. "But it was obviously serious enough to make the Kinders split town."

"Exactly," Sara said, jumping up again.

"Look, I'm sure there's a perfectly good explanation for all this," Danny replied. "I'm just not sure what it is—"

"I know this sounds weird," Sara cut in, her mind going a mile a minute. "But I'm gonna run and check on Anna real quick."

"What?"

"I know I'm being paranoid—"

"Just a little," Danny agreed. "I mean, she's got Brad with her."

"Oh, I know," she mumbled, slumping back down again.

Danny looked at his new wife, her face filled with concern and said, "If it will make you feel better, I'll run over and check on Anna and Brad."

"You will?" Sara asked.

"Yes. But I'm not staying over there all night," he smiled.

"Thanks, I know this is silly. Just run over, say hello, and then hurry back home to me."

"You got it," Danny grinned. "I'll be right back."

*   *   *

"Goodnight, Eddie," Joanne Simpson said to the Barn Yard Inn's final customer of the night. "Take care."

Tom walked out from the kitchen and asked, "Is that it?"

"That's the last one," she replied. "Except for old George here."

"That's me," George grumbled.

"Well, what do you say, George?" Joanne asked. "You wanna call it a night?"

"All right," George sighed. "I'm leaving."

Joanne, feeling sorry for him, said, "Awe, if you want you can stay until Tom and I are finished cleaning up, say, another twenty minutes."

"Great," George said, obviously relieved. "Thanks, Joanne."

"Sure," Joanne smiled. "Come on, Tom, let's get these last few dishes done."

"You're the boss," Tom said as he held open one of the swinging doors for her. "After you."

"Why, thank you," she laughed.

"No problem," Tom smiled.

"Give me a break," George muttered.

"You know," Tom said, after he was sure they were out of earshot. "He really seems terrified to go outside."

"I've noticed that," Joanne agreed. "I don't know what happened to him tonight, but it sure had a severe affect on him."

"You ain't kidding," Tom said. "Hey, ah, Joanne?"

"Yeah?" She replied as she filled the sink with soapy water.

"I was wondering, um, that maybe sometime we could—"

The bells above the front entrance chimed, interrupting Tom's hopeful date proposal.

Joanne looked at Tom as she quickly dried her hands and said, "What was that? Did George leave?"

"I don't know," he replied. "Let's go see."

The pair went back through the swinging double doors to the bar. "Oh, hi," Joanne said, surprised.

Standing there, holding a gun and looking extremely pale, was Allan Parker.

*   *   *

"Cash or credit?" the gas station attendant asked. The name on his shirt read GARY.

"Credit."

"Can I have your card, sir?" Gary asked.

"Sure," the driver answered, handing him an American Express card.

"Thanks."

"You're welcome," the man replied, praying silently that Gary wouldn't look in the back section of his Escape. He had failed to realize until now that he had neglected to cover up the objects that now lay open for anyone to gaze upon.

"Where are you heading?" Gary asked.

"Promised Land."

"Oh, that's a nice town," Gary said. "Peaceful."

"Let's hope so," the driver replied.

"Huh?"

"Oh, um, nothing," he replied. "Nothing at all."

*   *   *

"This must be the place," Danny said as he pulled into a paved driveway. As he got out of the car, he looked up and whistled. The house was three stories, and it seemed that the lights were on in almost every room. There were tall, curtainless windows on the bottom floor, stretching almost from floor to ceiling. From where he stood, he could see into what appeared to be their dining room. It was very well furnished from one end of the room to the other, with a large oak table in the center.

Danny went up the walkway to a small porch and rang the doorbell. There was no answer. As he waited, he suddenly remembered that Anna said they were going to go swimming. So dropping off the porch, he walked to his right. Past the driveway, there was a small walkway that led around back. Being a landscaper himself, Danny admired the oriental trees lining the house amongst the red mulch.

When he first reached the backyard, he didn't notice anything out of the ordinary. The path led him to the patio. That area, with its grill, glass table set and built-in Jacuzzi, was in perfect order and undisturbed. Then, he walked out into the yard toward the pool.

He was three quarters of the way there when saw something lying along side the pool. "What's that?" He jogged the rest of the way over and then stopped short.

Danny could feel his dinner rushing up his esophagus and he didn't even have time to finish kneeling before he started vomiting. There, in front of him, was the lower half of a body. "Oh God, what—" Then he saw the pool, and he shrieked loudly in spite of himself. "Anna?"

Danny stood up, his mind spinning so quickly that he thought he was going to pass out. After a moment, his vision cleared. That's when he saw the oak tree, and the body lying near it. "Oh no," Danny said as he sprinted past the pool and out into the large yard. "Brad!"

Upon reaching this body, Danny saw that it was so badly chewed up that he could only assume that the body was Anna's date. Danny's mind fought frantically to keep him under control and not to freak out. Just as he turned to leave he heard something. Just a low rumble at first, but then as it grew louder he instinctively knew what it was . . . a growl.

Danny turned and looked in all directions. All he saw was the house, the pool and in the distance on all sides, the forest. He was completely out in the open in the well-lit yard. The only thing close to him was the huge tree and the remains of Brad Thompson. After a moment the noise died and silence filled the air again. No crickets, no owls or anything else one might expect to hear this time of night in the mountains. Just silence. After cautiously searching his surroundings, he took a step back toward the house. Instantly the growl started again. Danny froze in his tracks and, without moving his legs, turned his head and looked behind him . . . to find nothing. Danny felt the urge to run, but he had the feeling that that would be a deadly mistake. He wasn't the wilderness type of guy, but he had heard that running in a situation like this never went well. But he also knew he couldn't just stand there either. So, he took another step. Then, another. After his fourth step the low growl turned into a loud roar.

Frantically Danny turned around and looked in every direction: left, right, back and forward and still saw nothing. Then, he slowly looked up. About halfway up the massive tree there was a large dark form nestled against the trunk. Danny couldn't tell what it was, for all he could see was a gleaming, almost piercing red eye glaring down at him.

He turned slowly back around. Danny Walker couldn't remember any other time in all his life when he was this terrified. But he had to think and he had to think fast. Just for a moment, his mind drifted to Sara. For a split second he thought about what it would be like to never see her again. And with that thought in mind, he broke into a sprint.

*　　*　　*

"Why, Allan," Joanne said, stepping out from the kitchen. "What brings you here this late?"

"Geeze," Tom said. "You look like you seen a ghost."

"Or a monster," George said, looking Allan over.

Allan walked over and took the stool next to George. As he slumped down, he looked George Stine straight in the eye and nodded. "Yes, George, you could say that."

"Could say what?" Tom asked.

"A monster," Allan said casually over his shoulder.

"And did you see this monster, Allan?" Tom queried.

"No," Allan replied. "Because if I had, I wouldn't be sitting here talking to you now."

*   *   *

Danny had run five yards when the roar became almost deafening. After a moment, there came a thunderous crash as the creature sprung from the tree to the ground. As he ran Danny couldn't help but think, *that thing was at least thirty feet in the air.*

Because he took the creature by surprise, Danny had put a good fifteen yards in between them. He sprinted past the pool and straight toward the patio. Even though he ran with all his might, he could tell that the monster was quickly gaining on him. Frantically he reached for the doorknob to the glass back door of the house and hoping it was unlocked, turned it.

The door swung inward and Danny raced into the house, through the kitchen and into the dining room, which he knew would lead to the front door and to his car. Seconds after he reached the dining room, the creature rammed itself full speed through the glass door and into the kitchen.

Danny reached the front door and yanked it open. Once on the porch, he quickly slammed the door closed and stumbling down the steps, made his way to his car. Danny jumped in and threw the car into reverse and peeled out of the driveway. Just as he reached the road, the dining room windows shattered as the creature erupted out onto the lawn.

Punching the gear into drive, Danny sped off down the small gravel road. He quickly stole a glance in his rearview mirror and saw that the creature had reached the road. It watched Danny for a moment, but then disappeared into the foliage. "Okay," he stuttered, "Calm down. It's over. Whatever that thing was, it's gone. Go get Sara, and join the Kinders in getting out of Dodge."

*   *   *

Sara opened the sliding glass door and stepped out onto the deck. It was a beautiful night, fairly cool with a light breeze and not a cloud in the sky. She looked up to see a full moon staring down at her. Then she glanced down at her watch. "Hmm," she murmured. "Ten-thirty. You've been gone almost a half-hour, Mr. Walker. Anna must be talking your ear off." As she turned to reenter the house a strange noise halted her. Turning back around, she squinted downhill toward the road. It was way too dark to see anything but she could definitely hear it. *What is that?* Sara thought. *A horse?* It sounded like something was galloping toward her direction on the red clay and gravel road. A moment later, something came into view. Sara gasped loudly at the size of the animal she saw in front of her. Apparently she gasped too loudly. The large animal slowly turned its head toward her. She still didn't know what it was, but it had two different colored eyes.

A split second later, those eyes were bounding quickly toward her.

Chapter Thirty-Eight

"So you didn't see this monster?" Tom Reimer asked, obviously being skeptical.

Allan shook his head. "Nope."

"Then how do you know there is one?" Tom asked again.

"My deputy Bill Darley saw it," Allan answered matter-of-factly.

"And how do you know he wasn't lying?" Tom shot back.

"Oh, he wasn't lying," Allan answered. After he said this, Allan angrily thought to himself, *snap out of it! You have a lot of work to do, a lot of people to tell. Don't freeze up, not again. Don't let other people suffer the way Bill did, the way your old partner Jake did. Stay in control!*

"Well?"

"Well what?"

"Well, how do you know he wasn't lying?" Tom asked.

Finally, Allan pulled himself together. "Because," he exclaimed, jumping up. "He couldn't have lied because his upper half of his body was two yards away from his lower half!"

"What?" Joanne stammered. "Bill's dead?"

"You could say that," Allan retorted. "And so is his buddy Charlie."

"His poor mother—" Joanne started to say.

"Yeah, well," Allan interrupted her. "We need to warn as many people as we can. Go to the homes of people we know are still here, tell them to stay indoor or to get out of town, either one. I'm going to call the state police and get them out here ASAP."

"What is it?" George asked. "Really?"

"Honestly," Allan said. "I don't know."

*   *   *

Sara screamed and ran back into the house, slamming and locking the sliding glass door. She then quickly pulled the curtain across the door and took several steps back. Her heart was pounding so fast and loud that she was sure the creature could hear it. Several moments went by with no commotion. *Maybe it ran away,* she thought.

Sara walked quietly toward the curtain. Once there, she slowly reached out and grabbed it. Hesitating only for a moment, she pulled the curtain back. As she did so, a giant paw smashed the door, showering her with shards of glass. Sara fell back and landed hard on her back. Temporarily dazed, she watched as the large animal peered through the doorway. The bright light shining from the nearby lamp exposed the creature in full. All Sara could do was cry as it slowly made its way through the door. Some parts fur, other parts reflected off the lamp as if they were scales. Even with its mouth closed, huge teeth stuck out in both directions. *Come on!* Sara's inner voice demanded. *Get up!* She knew she would never reach the kitchen in time; it was too far away. What was she going to do? Then she remembered something Danny did yesterday when they first arrived at the house.

Sara jumped to her feet just as the creature finished making its way through the door. It eyed her suspiciously for a moment and then with a loud roar, it lunged at her.

Sara quickly turned and dove headfirst through the once-was window that led to the small bedroom Danny had stuck his head through the day before. Landing hard on her stomach, she quickly turned over in time to see the creature's head appear through the opening as it rammed the wall.

The whole house shook, sending pictures and other knick-knacks to the floor. It roared angrily as the wall stayed in tact. Sara's own face was only a foot from the creature's. For a moment it just stared at her. It seemed to almost study her. Then it surged forward, pushing as hard as it could against the wall. Sara jumped to her feet just as a huge crack started to appear across the wall. "Oh no," Sara moaned. She quickly turned and ran out the bedroom through the dining room and out the front door . . . just in time to see Danny running up the steep steps that led to the house.

"Sara! Are you okay? I saw the back door—"

"It's inside!" Sara cut in, crying hysterically. "I was outside and it just came running—"

"Never mind that," Danny exclaimed as he reached the top of the stairs. "Come on, let's get out of here!"

Just as Sara started down the porch steps the creature came pounding down the deck steps, obviously having given up on the wall.

"Sara!" Danny hollered. "Freeze!"

The creature walked into the middle of the yard-right between Danny and Sara. "Get back in the house," Danny whispered.

"No," Sara cried.

"Get back in, *now*!" Danny hissed.

The creature looked from Sara to Danny, and then back to Sara. It started toward Sara.

"No!" Danny screamed. He quickly bent down and picked up a large stone and flung it at the creature. It bounced off the creature's head with an almost metallic sound. "Over here!"

"Danny—no!"

"Hey!" he screamed, waving his arms. "Yo, you freak! Come and get me!" The creature turned and, with out hesitation, started toward Danny.

Danny turned and sprinted past the shed and the campfire site and headed toward his only hope of survival. The A-frame roof of the well entrance came quickly into view and Danny rolled right into it.

With the creature right behind him, he quickly swung his legs over the side and found the old ladder. He only went down two rungs when the ladder let out another terrible creak and before Danny knew it, the ladder buckled and broke off in the middle. As Danny was falling toward the cemented bottom of the well, he saw those red and yellow eyes gleaming down at him with hatred. Then nothing at all.

Part Three

Atonement
August 22nd

Chapter Thirty-Nine

"Danny?"

Only silence answered. "Danny?" This time a soft groan could be heard. "Danny, can you hear me?"

"Ouch," came the response from the bottom of the well. "S-Sara, what's, ah, happening? Where are you?"

"I'm up here," she replied. "Are you okay?"

"I'm a bit disoriented," he said as he stood up and slumped back against the wall. Then, as if a lightning bolt just jogged his memory, he frantically asked,

"Where is it?"

"Gone."

"Gone?"

"Yes," she paused. "At least I think so."

"You *think* so?" The well echoed.

"Yeah. After you fell, the thing stood there staring down at you for a minute or so. Then, without even looking back at me, it took off."

"How do you know it wasn't just hiding—"

"I waited for a couple of minutes to make sure—"

"Just minutes?" Danny exclaimed as he worried about his wife's lack of self-preservation.

"Here catch," Sara said as a coil of rope slithered its way down to Danny.

129

"Where'd you get this?"

"The shed."

"I can't believe you are risking your life like this—"

"Well, I had to do something," she retorted. "I couldn't just leave you down a well. Besides, if that thing came back I would have just jumped down there with you."

"Then we'd both would have been stuck!" Danny said.

"Well, at least we would have been together!" Sara snapped. "I've tied the other end of the rope to a large tree over by the shed. So quit your hollering and get up here before that thing really does come back!"

"Okay," Danny replied, tugging on the rope. Then, with what little strength he had, Danny started to climb up the rope.

Over the grunting and groaning that could be heard, Sara asked, "You okay?"

"Just like in gym class," Danny replied, using his sense of humor to try and keep his mind off the throbbing pain in the back of his head.

After another minute, Danny's hands appeared over the rim. Sara grabbed them and helped pull her husband the rest of the way out.

They both slumped to the ground, exhausted. After his breathing and heart rate slowed back down, Danny sat up. "We have to get help."

"Right," Sara agreed. Then, she paused. "Anna?"

"What?" Danny asked, still a little dazed.

"Did you see Anna?"

Danny lowered his eyes and slowly shook his head. "She didn't make it."

"What?" Sara said, not fully grasping the statement.

Danny raised his head and met her eyes. "I'm sorry."

Sara let out a loud sob and sank into her husband's chest. He hugged her back, but only for a moment. "We have to go."

"Okay," she managed to mumble.

"I don't know where to go," he said. "It's after eleven o'clock at night. I don't know which houses to go to—"

"The B.Y.I.," Sara blurted out. "Maybe Joanne's still there."

"Okay, let's go," Danny answered.

"Maybe she'll know how to get a hold of the park ranger," Sara said.

"They're gonna need more than that," Danny said as they made their way down the steep stairway to the Intrepid.

Chapter Forty

"You don't know what it is?" Tom asked, surprised.

"Was it a bear?" Joanne asked.

"If we were in grizzly country, I'd consider it a possibility," Allan answered, still holding his deputy's shotgun, Old Betsy. "But even then . . ." His voice trailed off as he pictured the tent scene again.

"George," Joanne said. "I owe you an apology. I'm sorry I didn't believe you before."

"Me too," Tom chimed in.

"It's okay," George said with a wave of his hand. "I probably wouldn't have believed me either."

"Am I missing something?" Allan asked, confused. "What happened while I was up in the mountain?"

George quickly explained what had happened to him earlier that night. When he was done, Allan muttered, "Great. I was hoping it would stay in the deep foliage and not even bother coming into town."

"Oh, it bothered," George said.

"So what do we do now?" Tom asked.

"Well," Allan replied. "Who do we know is still up here?"

"The Hendersons," Joanne answered.

"The Wilsons," Tom added.

"I'm pretty sure the Olsons are still in town," George said, scratching his head.

"Okay, okay," Allan said. "Let's get into our cars and go as fast as possible to everyone we know for sure is still up here. In the process, I'll stop by the station and phone in the state police and I guess the, ah, animal control people."

"Animal control? The state police? Man, call in the freakin' marines!" George exclaimed.

"Everybody set?" Allan asked.

"Sure," Joanne said. "Sounds like a plan."

"Yeah, a bad one," George said as they got ready to go.

*　　*　　*

The green metal sign reflected brightly off the Escape's headlights. It read: WELCOME TO PROMISED LAND.

"Okay," the driver said nervously. "Now what do I do?"

He had planned this moment for some time. He knew he should have waited until daylight, but he couldn't bear to sit at home a minute longer without knowing the truth.

"With any luck, this will all have been a waste of time." Even as he said those words, his heart began to sink. Something told him it was worse than he had originally imagined. Much worse . . .

Chapter Forty-One

"Okay then," Allan said as he grabbed Old Betsy and headed toward the door. "Let's get going." Then, he stopped and pulled out his .45 pistol. "George, here. You and Joanne ride together."

He handed George the gun. "Do you know how to use that?"

"Of course," George smirked, clicking the safety off and on. Having the gun seemed to strengthen him somehow. "Let's do this."

Allan turned and was about to push on the door when it suddenly swung open. "Whoa!" he cried as two young people raced into the bar. "What's going on?"

Joanne blinked. "Sara? Danny? What are you doing here?"

"Hey," Danny said. "You found the park ranger."

"Found me?" Allan asked.

"Joanne!" Sara sobbed, running over to her. "Come on, we have to get out of here and get help!"

"Hold it a minute," Allan said, rising up his hand. "What happened?"

"Look," Danny said. "We know this is going to sound crazy, but something is—"

Suddenly the long windows to the left of the door exploded as the creature crashed through. It landed heavily on top of a table set, collapsing it instantly to the floor.

The six of them all screamed at once.

"What is *that*?"

"Oh no!"

"It's here!"

"George shoot it!" Joanne screamed.

George raised the gun and pulled the trigger. *Click! Click!* "The safety!" Allan yelled as he started to raise the shotgun. He was halfway up when his arms suddenly felt like weights. Everything seemed to slow down, almost as if he was watching the scene in slow motion. *Come on!* He thought. *Don't freeze! Not now! You vowed you never would again!*

Instantly snapping out of it, he raised the gun and fired. The round found its way into the wall two inches from the creature's head.

With lightning speed, the creature sprinted toward the frightened group. It picked out whom it wanted and, standing on its hind legs, lunged for her.

*　　*　　*

He drove slowly down the main road, searching for any signs of life. He knew it was late but he hoped that something, anything, would still be open.

He drove past the deserted beach, the Mountain Market and the local church. Nothing. Then, up ahead, he saw lights. "Bingo," he said with a small glimmer of hope. "Maybe it's not too late."

*　　*　　*

Joanne Simpson just stood there, frozen. She stared up at the enormous beast that stood before her. Its mouth opened, revealing hundreds, if not *thousands* of razor sharp teeth. Then, it came for her.

"Joanne! No!" Tom Reimer cried. Running as fast as he could, he pushed Joanne out of the way. She landed hard on the wooden floor.

The creature, already in motion, simply changed its target. Tom didn't have time to react. Its massive jaws grabbed him by the face and lifted him high off the ground.

"Tom! *No!*" Joanne howled in a voice she didn't recognize.

Tom let out a high-pitched scream as the creature tossed its head back and forth, flinging blood everywhere.

Then with one mighty jerk, Tom's body went flying across the room, the upper part of his face still clinging to the creature's mouth.

"Ahh!" George screamed and opened fire. The first few slugs penetrated the creature's stomach, causing it to drop back down to all fours. The rest of the bullets went ricocheting off the creature's back and shoulders.

"What?" George cried and pulled the trigger again. *Click!* "Oh no—I'm out!"

Allan raised the shotgun and fired. Sparks flew as the slug nailed the beast's right shoulder blade. "Huh?" *What's that thing made of?*

It did appear, however, to have stunned the creature. It took a step back and warily looked at Allan. Then, with a mighty roar, it started toward him.

"Quick!" Joanne yelled, jumping to her feet. "Into the kitchen!"

The group quickly rushed through the swinging double doors. Allan was the last to go through. As he did, he quickly turned and got off another shot. This one grazed the creature's right hind leg, causing it to slightly stumble.

"Allan! Come on!" Joanne exclaimed, standing by a very thick steel door. "In the freezer!"

Allan hurried in and Joanne slammed the door shut. A split second later, there came a thunderous vibration as the creature rammed the door.

"Oh no!" Sara cried.

It rammed the door again, leaving large bubble-like dents in the door. It hit it a third time.

"No," Joanne said. "It can't! That's almost a foot of pure steel!"

The creature hit it several more times, leaving many more large dents. But, the door held firm. Then silence filled the room.

For twenty minutes no one spoke a word. They were all too stunned. Joanne wept quietly. Allan was examining the door. Danny and Sara held each other while George stared down at his feet.

Then, the silence was broken. "Tom," Joanne whispered. "He saved my life."

"He did a very brave thing," Allan said, turning away from the door.

"It should have been me," Joanne sobbed. "It should be me out there."

"No," Sara said. She quickly walked over to Joanne and hugged her. "No, don't say that."

"Do you think it's gone?" George asked. He took a quick look around. They were in a rectangular room that George guessed was no more than ten by twelve. Metal racking that stretched from floor to ceiling covered the entire room, with narrow aisles in between each row. Frozen foods of every kind lined the shelves on the racking. George coughed and watched his breath float by him. "It's freezing in here."

"I'd rather be freezing than dead," Danny said, shivering despite himself.

"Well, do you think it's gone?" George asked again.

"I doubt it," Danny answered. "It's very persistent."

"How would you know?" George retorted.

"Call it a hunch," Danny said, not wanting to tell them that more lives had already been lost. They had enough to deal with.

"What is that thing?" Joanne asked. "I mean, did you see its eyes?"

"I don't know," Allan answered truthfully. "It resembled a bear, but—"

"But no bear can have bullets bounce off it like Superman," George finished the sentence.

"Yeah, it has some kind of armor," Allan agreed.

"Except for its stomach," Sara piped in. "When it was still standing up, George, you nailed it twice."

"That's right," George said. "Those bullets didn't reflect off, did they?"

"Good. At least it has a weakness," Danny said.

"Okay great," George grunted. "Can we go now? I can't feel my legs anymore and the walls are closing in all around me."

"No, we can't go yet," Joanne said softly.

"Huh?" George snorted. "Why not?"

"Because there's no door handle on this side," Allan answered, turning back toward the door. "It's locked from the other side."

"Oh, that's just great!" George exclaimed. "Now what do we do? Freeze to death? How could you—"

"We had to do something!" Joanne screamed shrilly. "It would have killed all of us!"

"She's right," Sara said. "Back off, George."

"At least we're still alive," Allan said.

"But for how long?" George asked. "We won't last more than—"

"We'll last a lot longer now than we would have if it wasn't for Joanne," Danny snapped. "You could be dead right *now*, George."

That comment sent a chill down George's already freezing spine. "You're right," George sighed. "Look, I'm sorry. I'm just slightly claustrophobic—"

"It's okay," Joanne said. "We're all scared."

George nodded in agreement. Then the room was silent again. But it didn't last long. *Swoosh.* "What was that?" Sara whispered.

"Oh no," Joanne sobbed. "That was the swinging doors. It's back."

Chapter Forty-Two

They all waited in horrified silence, their hearts in their throats. *Thump!*

"Oh no," Joanne whispered. *Thump!*

"It's right outside the door," Allan hissed.

They all listened intensely. Then, a voice floated to them through the thick door. "Ah, hello?"

For a moment nobody answered, too paralyzed with fear to comprehend that it wasn't the creature on the other side of the door.

"Is anybody in there?"

Then all at once, they started yelling.

"Yes, we're in here!"

"Be careful out there!"

"Help, we're locked in!"

Click! The damaged steel door slowly swung open. The huddled group all stared at the tall lanky man in the red baseball cap who just released them from their frozen haven.

"Are you okay?" the man asked.

"Yes," Allan answered. "For the most part."

"Who are *you*?" Joanne croaked.

"Me? I'm, ah, Jim. Jim Hoffer," the stranger answered.

"Who?" George snorted.

"Are you sure you are all okay?" Jim asked.

"We were attacked!" Joanne cried.

"By some monster!" Sara added.

"A monster?" Jim asked. "What did it look like?"

"Well," Allan said. "It *looked* like a bear. Well, sort of, but—"

"But it was huge!" Joanne cut in.

"We really don't know what it was," Sara said.

"Oh, it *was* a bear," Jim said matter-of-factly.

"It was?" Allan raised his eyebrows. "Tell me, Mr., ah—"

"Hoffer. But call me Jim."

"Okay, Jim, how exactly do you know it was a bear? And how is it you happened to find us back here this late at night?"

Jim paused, as if in deep thought. "Okay, let me start at the beginning. How about you all come out of the freezer and warm up."

"Is it safe?" Joanne asked.

"Yes, I think so," Jim replied. "I didn't see the, ah, monster. But your bar is a mess."

The group made their way out of the freezer and into the kitchen. "Brrr," George said, shivering. "I'm still freezing."

"Okay," Allan said, looking tentatively toward the swinging doors. "Let's hear your story."

"All right. Like I said, my name is Jim Hoffer and I am an employee, or rather former employee of Intech Pharmaceutical Company."

"Intech?" Joanne's eyes narrowed. "That big company over in Allentown?"

"Correct," Jim responded.

"What do you mean by former employee?" Allan asked.

"Two days ago I was fired," he answered.

"Why?" Danny asked.

"The reasons they gave me were silly," Jim said, a hint of anger in his voice. "Insubordination, or something along those lines. But the real reason was because I knew too much."

"Knew too much?" Allan asked. "Tell me, Jim, what exactly did you do when you worked for Intech?"

"They had me doing odd jobs for them at the research lab here in the mountain—"

"Whoa," Allan said, stopping him. "What research lab?"

"The one Intech didn't want anyone to know about," Jim said. "Originally they said it was a lab designed to research the breakdown of cancer cells in the hopes of learning new ways to battle the disease. But it became something totally different."

"On *my* mountain?" Allan exclaimed.

"No," Jim answered. "It's actually outside your jurisdiction. It's way up the mountain. Anyway, they had me doing general maintenance, moving things, trash removal and things like that. I knew I wasn't making a career out of it, but it was paying the bills."

"So what made you suspicious? What were they up to?" Joanne asked.

"Well, I knew they were doing research on a drug called Thalidomide. And I knew that it was outlawed for use on humans, because it had been notorious for causing birth defects."

"I remember hearing something about that," Danny said. "My mom used to work in a hospital."

"Right. Anyway, I would hear things being said by the technicians when I was working around the lab. I don't have a science background, but I overheard a lot this one day, enough to put some things together."

"They were trying to research the way Thalidomide affects DNA by experimenting with animals. I don't really know what types of animals they were experimenting with, I only know about the small ones in the lab. But I overheard a rumor one day while I was cleaning up a lab spill."

"What was the rumor?" George asked, intrigued by the story.

"That they had larger animals on the other side of the lab," Jim said. "It was restricted, I never saw that section. But from the pieces of conversation I overheard, I found out they were doing science fiction stuff."

"Science fiction?" Allan asked.

"Yeah, you know. Altering embryos of the animals that were fertilized in a test tube, just to find out what would happen to the DNA of the offspring."

"That's horrible!" Joanne said.

"They were combining Thalidomide with other drugs and subjecting the offspring to high amounts of radiation. Then they would give the animals some kind of compound to see if they could prevent cancer from radiation. I don't know what went wrong, but I believe they started out with good intentions."

"The road to hell is paved with good intentions," Joanne said.

"Yeah," Jim sighed as he remembered saying that very phrase to Arnold Flanks, who, as far as Jim knew, still worked for Intech. "I read on a report they left in the lab that the compound they gave the animals was Potassium Iodide. I did some of my own research and found out that Potassium Iodide can block the thyroid gland from absorbing radioactive material. I read a lot about it. You can sort of measure how much radiation exposure a person or animal has had by the thyroid gland."

Jim slowly looked around at the five strangers staring back at him. "Anyway, this scientific mumbo jumbo was way over my head too so I wrote down some more information," he said, pulling a piece of paper out of his pocket.

He cleared his throat and began to read. "'The thyroid gland secretes thyroxine and triodthyronine which both have a powerful affect on the maturation rate and on the metabolism in general.'"

He paused and glanced up at his audience. No one spoke, so he continued. "'In fact, hyperthyroidism causes heart palpitations, nervousness, hyper excitability, restlessness, insomnia and emotional instability. In humans, physical or emotional stress could set off a crisis called thyroid storm, which can cause vasomotor collapse and death if not treated.'" He folded the paper and shoved it back in his pocket.

"You lost me, buddy," George said. "Was that English?"

"So you're saying this thing was created in a lab by Intech?" Allan asked sternly.

"I'm saying I think it's possible that a genetically altered embryo of a large animal, say a bear, was exposed to high amounts of radiation, creating a hyperthyroid state."

"Oh, is that all?" George smirked. "To think I was beginning to worry."

"I remember them saying something about a bear being caught," Jim continued. "They probably captured a female bear and used its artificial offspring to experiment on."

"How can they get away with that?" Sara asked.

Jim shook his head. "I don't know. But I do know one thing. Since its mother didn't nurture this creature, it has no normal instincts."

"What are you saying?" Allan asked, daring a peak out into the bar. All was still.

"I'm saying that it doesn't have the normal instincts that a regular bear should have. It has only emotional instability, hyper excitability and also a touch of insomnia. In other words, sir, you've got one large, angry bear."

Chapter Forty-Three

Silence hung heavy in the kitchen where just a little while ago laughter and the clanging of dishes had filled the air. Joanne closed her eyes. *This is all a horrible dream. When I open my eyes, I'll be home in bed. Then, I'll get up and come to work. Tom will behind the bar, smiling as always. Who knows? Maybe we'll go see a movie sometime . . .*

She opened her eyes. She saw Danny and Sara leaning against the large sink to her right. To her left she saw George, still rubbing his arms to get warm. And directly in front of her she saw Allan talking to Jim Hoffer.

"You answered my first question," Allan was saying. "Now for the second one. How did you happen to find us here this late at night?"

"I'll get to that soon," Jim said. "You see, before I was fired and roughly escorted out of the building in Allentown, I managed to get my hands on some very significant documents. These documents would put Intech in a very bad light."

"Good," Joanne said.

"I have those documents in my Escape outside," Jim continued. "Anyway, in these confidential documents I read about these larger animals—"

"But how did this thing get out?" George asked.

"Yeah, wasn't this lab of yours secure?" Allan asked as well.

"First off, it wasn't *my* lab. Secondly, it was very secure. It was a big building with thick walls—"

"Then how did it get out?" George asked again. "Did someone let it out?"

"No."

"Then how'd it get out?" George cried. "From the way you make it sound, you'd have to have a tank—"

"Or a tornado," Sara said quietly.

"What?" George said.

"An F-2 tornado," Sara said, louder this time.

"Bingo," Jim said. "It literally tore the place to shreds. Most of the animals inside were killed instantly. But some of the larger ones escaped."

"Larger *ones*?" Allan stammered. "There's more than one?"

"No—"

"What? Do I have a four-headed mutant deer running around too?" Allan exclaimed.

"No," Jim answered. "According to the documents, the company actually gathered together and sent out a team to hunt down and eliminate those animals. They were successful in their attempts, save one."

"Our friend," Allan said.

"Yes, EBB-5," Jim said.

"E-B-who?" George asked.

"Experimental Black Bear number five," Jim said. "That's its name, according to what I've read."

"So they just let it go?" Danny asked.

"No, not entirely," Jim answered. "They sent a secondary team to find the bear when the first team couldn't."

"And?" George snapped.

"And they were never seen again," Jim said sternly. "The company covered it up. The way they cover everything up. Anyway, with the building being destroyed, the company called the project a failure and shut it down. The company hoped that the bear would run off somewhere and die, I guess."

"Well, it didn't," George snapped. "So how does all this help us?"

Jim lowered his head. "It's supposed to help you understand—"

"Oh, I understand," Allan butted in. "I understand perfectly. Your company, in the name of humanity creates this . . . thing. Then they lose it and decide to just cover it up."

"Sounds like the plot of a bad horror movie," George grunted.

Jim said nothing. "Look," Allan sighed. "I know none of this is your fault—"

"Listen," Jim said, interrupting. "I have all the evidence I need to shut down Intech for good."

"Great!" George yelled. "I still don't see how that helps *us*!"

"Why'd you come here tonight?" Joanne managed to ask.

"Before I went public with this, I needed to know if the bear was still alive. For all I knew it could have stayed deep in the mountain somewhere. But I had a really bad feeling—"

"So you drove to the nearest town to see if anything was going on," Allan finished his sentence. "You were coming to warn us."

"Yes," Jim said.

"But how does that help—" George began to say again.

"It helps you," Jim cut in. "Because I came prepared for the worst. I have some guns—"

"They're useless," George smirked.

"Huh?"

"It has some kind of armor," Allan said. "Everywhere but its stomach."

"Really? That's . . . different. Well if guns don't work I also have enough explosives to blow it to kingdom come."

"Explosives?" Joanne echoed.

"Well," George said, surprised. "Now we're talking."

"It's set to a timer," Jim said. "But be careful, once you set the timer, it can't be turned off."

"So," George said sarcastically. "All we have to do is get that bad boy to roll over on his tummy and strap the explosives to him. Simple."

"Right," Jim said seriously. "If the rest of him is an armor of some kind, then an explosion at the right spot would ricochet throughout his whole body—"

"Killing it," Danny said with determination.

"Right again," Jim said. "But we'd better hurry."

"Why?" Sara asked.

"Yeah, what's the rush?" George agreed.

"According to the documents," Jim said. "They caught EBB-5's mother in early June."

"June?" Allan stammered. "But today is only August 22nd!"

"Correct," Jim replied.

"You mean to tell us that this thing is only *three months old*?"

"Yes," Jim answered. "And that's not the bad news."

"Oh boy," George snorted.

"Allan, when would you say that the average male black bear reaches sexual maturity?"

"Between five and six years old," Allan said. "Hold up, are you saying—"

"I'm saying that this thing is growing a thousand times faster than a normal black bear. Soon, it will start looking to mate."

"Then there would be more of those things?" Joanne croaked.

"Quite possibly," Jim said soberly.

"It's already eliminating its competition," Allan said. "The other day Bill found a slaughtered male black bear."

"You knew about this thing?" George suddenly accused. "And you didn't tell us?"

"No, I didn't know," Allan protested. "We had found some deer—"

"My friend Henry is probably dead because you knew and didn't tell us!" George roared.

"No, I didn't!" Allan screamed back. "Okay, George? I didn't. I didn't know that a lab-induced mutant bear was running around my town! All right?"

"Okay, okay," Sara said, stepping in between the heated men like a referee at a boxing match. "Let's cool it guys, this isn't helping things any."

"Let's try and figure out what we're going to do," Danny suggested.

"Agreed," Allan said, cooling down. "Let's see, an average black bear can run over thirty miles per hour, climb trees like a squirrel and attack quite effectively if provoked."

"So?" George snorted.

"So magnify that times ten!" Joanne said hysterically. "How are we going to stop this . . . killing machine?"

"First things first," Allan said. "We are not going to do anything foolish. "I'm going to use the phone by the bar and call in some major help."

Allan started toward the phone but stopped when the lights suddenly went out. "Oh no!" Joanne cried.

"It's pitch black in here!" George cried. "What a time for the power to go out!"

"I'm not so sure it did," Allan said.

"What do you mean?" Danny asked.

"The average black bear is highly intelligent," Allan said through the darkness. "Again, magnify that by ten."

"Are you saying the *bear* cut the power?" George exclaimed.

As an answer, a loud angry roar shook the night.

Chapter Forty-Four

For a moment no one moved. Then a small circle of light broke the darkness. "I sure am glad I brought along this flashlight this afternoon," Allan said. He cautiously made his way to the swinging doors. Pushing one open, he shone his light into the bar.

The light illuminated the bar itself, some stools and the front entrance. Turning to his left he saw the smashed table set and—*what was that?*

What was that quick flash of yellow? Was it just the reflection from the broken windows or was it an angry glare from a single distorted yellow eye?

"Anything?" Joanne hissed from the kitchen.

Allan brought the light back to the spot by the broken windows. Nothing was there. "No," he replied.

"So what now?" George asked loudly.

"Quiet!" Joanne retorted.

"I'm going to try the phone by the bar," Allan answered. "We need to get some serious help." He lifted the partition between the counters and made his way to the far right side of the bar. He picked up the receiver, listened and then quickly slammed it down. "Great," he muttered.

"What?" George called out.

"Line's dead," Allan said.

"Did our brilliant bear do that too?" George snorted.

"I don't know," Allan said as he made his way back to the group. "I have to get to the ranger station and see if that phone is working. It might be the whole town."

"That wouldn't be surprising," Joanne said.

"Doesn't anybody have a cell phone?" Jim asked.

"No," Joanne answered. "No need for one. No matter how good your phone is nobody gets reception in this part of the mountain. You'd have to drive at least to Canadensis."

"Oh," was Jim's response.

"So what do we do now?" George asked. "If that thing is still out there, it might chase us back into the freezer."

"Yeah," Sara agreed. "And this time there wouldn't be anybody to open the door for us—we'd be trapped."

"If we can get to my Escape, we can all climb in and go to this ranger station of yours," Jim said. "Then we could develop a game plan—"

"And get help," Danny chimed in.

"Exactly."

"Sounds like a plan," George said. "Let's get outta here."

"Okay," Allan said. "I'll lead the way with the shotgun. We'll go quietly, single-file. We'll jump in the Escape, arm ourselves and go get help for this town. Everybody ready?"

Everyone numbly nodded. "Okay then, let's go."

*   *   *

It waited in perfect stillness. Having poor eyesight, it depended greatly on its sense of smell. And it could clearly smell them now. *Prey.* They were coming closer.

Chapter Forty-Five

Allan cautiously pushed open the swinging doors with Old Betsy. Next came Joanne, holding the flashlight. Danny and Sara came after her, followed by George and then Jim Hoffer.

As they walked, George whispered over his shoulder. "Hey, Jim? What kind of explosives you got out there?"

"Four sticks of dynamite secured by duct tape," Jim responded. "They're fastened to a timer that is powered by a nine-volt battery. The problem is once the timer is set, the only way to shut it off would be to unscrew the compartment with a tiny screwdriver and take out the battery."

"Pretty time consuming," George said.

"Right," Jim agreed. "And that's if you had the right size screwdriver handy, which by the way, I forgot to bring. That's why I said earlier that the timer couldn't be shut off."

"Okay," Allan said. "We're almost to the entrance." Their footsteps crunched softly over the broken glass and debris caused by the earlier actions of the man-made monster.

Joanne couldn't help but look to her left into the dining area where Tom's body was thrown. Luckily, it was too dark to see any of the gruesome details.

"All right," Allan whispered, stopping next to the front entrance.

"We'll walk, not run as quietly as we can to Jim's Escape. If that thing is still out there, I'll hold it off as long as I can with the shotgun."

"Remember to aim for the stomach," Joanne said.

"Right. With any luck, we'll all be at the ranger station in five minutes," Allan replied as he slowly opened the door, being careful not to sound the chimes above them.

Stepping outside onto the gravel, he almost expected to be instantly attacked. Yet nothing moved. Joanne followed, shining the light in all directions. "Maybe it's gone," she whispered.

Danny and Sara stepped out next, followed by George Stine. "Let's get out of here," he mumbled. "Where's the Escape?"

"Over to the left," Jim said, grabbing his keys from his pocket. The vehicle was about thirty yards away, at the other end of the building. "All the weapons and those incriminating documents are in the back."

"Good," Joanne said. "Let's go."

The Escape's taillights blinked as Jim hit the remote entry. "With your testimony and those documents, Intech is finally going to pay for their sins," he said with the slightest of smiles.

"It will be our pleasure," Joanne said.

"It certainly will," George agreed, thinking briefly of his friend Henry Watson.

"Ready?" As he motioned Allan to lead the way, something dripped onto Jim's shoulder. As a reflex, Jim reached up and touched his shoulder. He rubbed the substance between his fingers. *What is this?* Then it came to him. *Saliva.* "Oh no," he whispered softly as he slowly looked up.

Before he even finished, the razor-sharp claws already pierced his sides and began to lift him up. Even as Jim let out a hysterical scream, he thought: *perched on the lower portion of the roof . . . clever.*

"Jim!" George yelled and grabbed onto Jim's dangling legs. "Let him go!"

Danny joined in the macabre tug-of-war between George and the creature. "No!"

"Out of the way!" Allan yelled as he made his way back to the struggle. "Joanne! Shine the light up!"

Joanne obeyed and the horrible scene was brought into full view. The creature was crouched on the edge of the roof, struggling to keep its balance and hoist up Jim at the same time. The top part of Jim was covered in blood as the creature was clawing and biting him.

Allan raised the shotgun and carefully took aim, trying to find a spot that was clear of Jim. Then, he fired. The bullet pierced the armor of the creature's left shoulder. With a roar of surprise and pain, it let Jim Hoffer go. Allan fired a second blast but the creature had turned and scurried farther back on the roof.

"Jim!" Danny cried as he cradled the man's head in his now blood-soaked lap. "Come on!"

Allan kneeled down by them. "Oh God," he whispered. Allan knew with one quick glance that Jim's wounds were fatal.

Jim slowly looked up at Danny. Then he turned toward George and Allan. "Make them pay," he choked. "*Kill this thing and make them pay.*"

"Hang in there, Jim!" George exclaimed. "You can do it!"

But, it was too late. Jim was gone. Danny closed his eyelids and laid his head softly on the ground. "Where are his keys?"

Allan and George exchanged glances. "He must have dropped them!" George said, dropping to his knees. "Joanne, over here with the light!"

"I know he unlocked the Escape, so they have to be close by," Allan said. As he said this, there came an angry, explosive roar. Everybody looked up. The sound seemed to have come from the left of them, where everyone else's vehicles happened to be parked.

"Well, we can't go that way," George said, searching the ground. "We only have one choice. They *have* to be here!"

Just then, another ear-piercing roar ripped the night in two. They all looked up again . . . and saw it. The creature was standing about fifty yards away, right next to Danny's Intrepid. It seemed to be eyeing them up. Eyeing them up with those angry, evil eyes.

"It hates us," Joanne whispered. "It knows humans are responsible for what has happened to it."

"Yeah, but it wasn't us!" George hissed.

"I don't think it cares," Sara replied.

It took several steps forward, then stopped. "Okay," Allan said. "Let's all start taking small steps backward toward the Escape."

"But we don't have the keys!" George said.

"I know," Allan replied calmly. "But it's better than standing out here like sitting ducks and besides . . . I only have one shot left."

"Gotcha," George said quickly and took a small step back.

"Slowly now," Allan said. "Maybe it will stay back. I think that last shot broke through, I think I hurt it."

*   *   *

The creature stood its ground and watched. It was slightly wary of them. This last encounter it experienced something unusual. It experienced pain. This feeling, however, was dull compared to the feeling of rage it was unintentionally programmed to feel.

It suddenly rose up on its hind legs and sniffed the air heavily, a mixture of snot and salvia flowing freely down its massive body. It stopped suddenly as it smelled something it was familiar with. The wonderful smell of *fear*. Then something in its mind triggered its deepest anger, its deepest hatred toward these . . . *things*. It knew what it must do.

Chapter Forty-Six

Everyone tensed as the creature stood up. "What's it doing?" Sara asked quietly.

"I don't know," Allan answered. "But I don't think it's good."

"Oh great," George mumbled.

"Start walking slowly back again," Allan ordered. "No matter what happens, don't stop. When you get to the Escape, grab whatever guns Jim had brought along and get ready."

They were about twelve yards away when the creature suddenly let out a vengeful roar and dropping back down to all fours, it charged full speed ahead.

"*Run!*" Allan screamed. The small group of five broke into a sprint toward the lone vehicle. "Hurry!"

As she ran, Sara tripped over a large stone and fell to the ground. Danny skidded to a stop and ran back and grabbed her. "Come on!" She quickly got to her feet and they darted back toward the Escape.

George was the first to reach the vehicle and flung open the rear hatch. In front of him sat two piles. One was a large stack of folders. The other was a small pile of handguns. And in the center was the dynamite.

Joanne came up behind him. "Hand me something!"

"No," George said. "Get in and get down."

"What?"

"Just do it! I'm not gonna let that thing get you!" George exclaimed.

"George—"

"*Now!*" he screamed.

Joanne ran quickly around and dove in the back seat. A moment later, Danny and Sara were by his side. "Here," George said, handing Danny a handgun. "Just start shooting. Sara, get in with Joanne."

"Huh?"

"Just do it!"

"I'm not leaving my husband!"

"Get in!" George exclaimed, slamming his fist down. After he did this, he suddenly heard a faint beeping sound. The three of them looked down in unison. George slowly moved his fist and saw a large, red digital timer. It read: 5:00 . . . 4:59 . . . 4:58 . . . 4:57 . . . 4:56 . . . 4:55 . . .

"Ut-oh," George said.

"Oh no!" Danny exclaimed. "The explosives! You hit the timer!"

"I can see that," George retorted.

"Turn it off!" Sara said.

"I can't," George replied. "It can't be turned off."

"What?" Sara cried.

"Get in," George said calmly.

"But—"

"Just do it," Danny said.

Sara started to protest, but then quickly turned and joined Joanne.

"Go on!" George shouted to Danny. "Go help Allan!"

Danny hesitated, then quickly turned and headed back toward the bar.

Ever since his beloved Edith died, George had been self centered and cold hearted toward everyone around him. It was finally time for atonement.

*   *   *

As the bear came quickly toward him, Allan calmly lowered to one knee and aimed. He waited until it was only ten yards away before firing his last shot. It struck the creature directly in the front left ankle.

It shrieked in pain and fell forward, landing on the ground with a tremendous thud. Allan jumped up and, like lightning, was on the creature. Grabbing the shotgun by the barrel, he started to slam the gun repeatedly into the bear's skull. "Die! Just die!"

With speed that Allan was not expecting, the creature whipped out its injured left paw and backhanded Allan, sending him flying into the side of the Barn Yard Inn.

The creature quickly stood up, and made its way over to the nearly unconscious Allan Parker. He slowly looked up into the beast's evil face.

It seemed to Allan, that the creature was almost smiling. "Go to hell," he whispered.

*   *   *

As the creature slowly opened its retched mouth, a series of gunshots rang out, hitting the creature in its metallic back.

It turned to see Danny Walker running at it, firing endlessly. *This one had escaped it several times tonight.* With a gleeful roar, it charged at him.

*   *   *

Danny skidded to a stop when the monster lurched forward. He was in the middle of the parking lot. There was no house to run to, no well to dive into. There was nowhere to hide. He raised his gun and fired until he heard the dreadful *click* of the empty chamber. In desperation, he tossed the gun at the beast and watched as it simply clanged off the creature's head. A moment later, it was on him.

It rammed Danny head on, sending him sailing through the air. He landed hard on his back, half his ribs breaking instantly. Then the creature, almost arrogantly, waltzed over to him and sprung up on its humungous hind legs. As Danny watched this, he quietly whispered, "Our Father who art in heaven, hallowed be thy name . . ."

"Hey!" A voice shouted. The creature started to lunge for Danny. *"Hey!"*

The creature stopped. Still on its hind legs, it slowly turned. Danny, half dazed, also looked up. Was he seeing things? A few yards behind them, stood George Stine. Danny did a double take. Through his blurred vision, Danny thought he saw the timer to the dynamite fastened around George's waist, attached through his belt loop.

"Yeah, you!" George exclaimed.

Danny pushed himself up on his elbows as the creature took a step toward George. "That's right, I've got something for you now you big, ugly *bastard!*"

Danny shook his head and finally saw the timer clearly. It read: 0:15 . . . 0:14 . . . 0:13 . . . 0:12 . . . 0:11 . . . 0:10 . . .

"George?" Danny called.

"Run, kid," George replied, without taking his eyes off the bear.

"But—"

"Run!" George yelled. 0:9 . . . 0:8 . . .

Danny got to his feet and started limping in the direction of the Escape.

The creature was coming for George, still walking upright. "That's right," he said quietly . . . 0:7 . . . 0:6 . . . 0:5 . . . "My, what a big belly you have." 0:4 . . . 0:3 . . . "The better to kill you with." Then like a flash, George reached out and grabbed the creature, almost hugging it, stomach to stomach. 0:2 . . . As the creature started to bring its claws down, George whispered one final word: *"Edith."* 0:1 . . .

Then there was a sudden ball of light. The thunderous blast knocked Danny clear off his feet again. He turned back to see a huge fireball, shooting large chunks of matter into the air. After a few seconds, the debris started crashing to the ground. As he tried to stand up, a large object landed directly in front of him. It was one of the creature's arms.

Suddenly hands grabbed him and hoisted him up. He turned to see Joanne and Sara's tear-stained faces. Then he turned and saw Allan walking limply towards them.

Sara draped Danny's arm around her neck for support. "George," Danny whispered softly. "He saved my life."

"He saved *all* our lives," Joanne choked.

Sara opened her mouth to say something, but then closed it. She was utterly speechless, for she was on an emotional roller coaster. Sara was saddened by George's death, yet in awe of his heroism. And mixed in at the same time, she was overjoyed to still be alive. Even more importantly, her husband was still alive. "I thought I lost you," she finally managed to say.

"I did too," Danny said through clenched teeth. "I thought I was never going to see you again."

"Yes," Allan said. "Thank you, I thought I was a dead man."

"Thank George," Danny replied. "He's the real hero."

The four stood silently as the fire dulled to a soft glow.

Epilogue

October 7th

T he late afternoon sun shone brightly over the vast mountain of trees, creating a blaze of orange, red and gold.

Sara Walker stood on the deck staring at the cross in the distance above the trees. It still seemed to glow. She glanced over at her husband. "You look funny without all those bandages wrapped around your waist."

"Yeah," Danny smiled. "They were multi-talented; it made a nice girdle."

Danny had spent almost two weeks in the hospital before finally being able to go home to his new wife. He had to take a leave of absence from his landscaping job while he recuperated, but now was finally back to one hundred percent.

They heard the familiar crunching of tires on the old clay and gravel road and looked down to see Allan Parker ride by in his tan Jeep Cherokee. He honked and waved as he drove by.

"After a while, we'll go see Joanne and have lunch at the B.Y.I.," Danny said.

"Sounds great," Sara smiled. "I'm going to go get ready."

"Okay," Danny said, flopping down into a lounge chair. "I think

I'll stay out here for a while. I'm enjoying the fresh air."

"Okay," Sara said as she slid open the new screen door and stepped inside. As she walked through the living room, she passed the television, which was turned on to the local news.

"At this time," a female reporter was saying. "It is now official: The biggest corporation on the eastern seaboard has been shut down. Intech Pharmaceutical Company has permanently closed its doors due to a decision by the Supreme Court today. The overwhelming evidence and the testimony of four key witnesses convinced the judge that illegal testing was being performed and that serious jail time is in the near future for all those involved in these repulsive experiments . . ."

Coming Soon!

FROSTBITE

Read on for an excerpt
from Frostbite

David Warren

Prologue

The great chain of rugged mountains known as the Rockies ranges from western North America all the way through to northeastern British Columbia. They form part of the great, or continental divide, which separates rivers draining into the Atlantic or Arctic Oceans from those flowing toward the Pacific Ocean.

The Great Basin and the Rocky Mountain Trench, a valley running from northwestern Montana to northern British Columbia, border the Rocky Mountains on the west, and by the Great Plains on the east.

The southern section of this two thousand mile chain, which includes the system's broadest and highest regions, runs straight through the state of Colorado. Seventy-five miles west of downtown Denver, nestled in the Ten Mile and Gore wilderness, sits the Whitman Mountain Resort.

With two thousand four hundred and thirty-five lift-served acres, Whitman Mountain is one of Summit County's largest ski and snowboard resort. Otherwise known as "Everyone's Favorite Place," Whitman owes this reputation to an award-winning trail system that enhances the mountain's unique geographic features, providing naturally separated terrain for expert, intermediate and beginner skiers and snowboarders.

Toward the bottom of the beginner's trail, about twelve yards into the forest, sits an abandoned cabin. Popularly known as "The Love

Shack," this small cabin is a frequent spot for couples with over zealous hormones. Since it consisted strictly of an old ripped cot and a small table set, people who have stumbled upon it in the past could think of nothing better to do inside its old, vacant walls. It had snowed heavily two nights before and there were now large snowdrifts reaching up toward the roof of the cabin.

Standing impatiently in front of the cabin now was Sally Rogers. Dressed in white leggings and an oversized pink parka, she let out an exaggerated sigh. "Jerk," she mumbled as she adjusted her white fluffy earmuffs.

Everyone knew of Alex Gunther's reputation. Sally was well aware that Alex got around with all the girls. And why wouldn't he? Alex was blonde, broad shouldered and muscular, with a dark tan even in the deadest of winter. He was one of the greatest ski instructors in the states today. But when it came to the women, Sally knew, he often showed them some of his other talents as well. *But,* she thought. *Our relationship is different. He really loves me. Me and only me.*

She glanced down at her watch and sighed again. Sally had been waiting since noon and it was now quarter to one. She would have waited inside the cabin, but it was colder in there then it was standing outside in the sun. *He must have been held up on a skiing lesson,* she reassured herself uncertainly. Then she shut her eyes and let out a long yawn. As she finished, she reopened her eyes and did a double take.

About ten yards in front of her, sat a rather large lump of snow. *Funny,* she thought, rubbing her eyes. *I don't remember that lump of snow being there before. I must be getting tired.*

She glanced up toward the sky. The sun was shining brightly, hardly a cloud in the sky. She almost seemed to be hypnotized by the glaring ball of light. Finally, she lowered her eyes back down. The lump of snow was now directly in front of her and less than a yard away.

"What?" She gasped. "How'd that happen?"

Then something stirred. Sally's eyes bulged and she opened her mouth to scream, but no sound came out. And for the first time today, Sally forgot all about Alex Gunther.

David Warren has written dozens of short stories and books and now lives in southern New Jersey with his wife, Suzanne, and their three children Katelyn, Matthew and Noelle.

www.ingramcontent.com/pod-product-compliance
Lightning Source LLC
Chambersburg PA
CBHW020338260626
47156CB00004B/1584